THE
PARIS APARTMENT

THE IRISH HEART SERIES,
BOOK 3

THE
PARIS APARTMENT

THE IRISH HEART SERIES, BOOK 3

BY JULIET GAUVIN

JULIET GAUVIN 🦋 LOS ANGELES

Published by Juliet Gauvin.
Available from Amazon.com and other retail outlets.
Available on Kindle and other devices.

www.julietgauvin.com

Scaoil do ghreim agus ar aghaidh leat ag eitilt!

Contents

To the readers who took this journey with me.

To the Unicorn, the Yeti, and the Dragon who made it happen.

THE
PARIS APARTMENT

THE IRISH HEART SERIES,
BOOK 3

Prologue: Fifteen Years Ago

"Wes, Mark, wait!" Beth called after them as she and Audre struggled to catch up.

They'd spent the weekend at Cambridge where Wes had been more than happy to play the host. Only Loryn had stayed behind in London.

Beth readjusted her book bag and followed her friends.

"When did you ladies become sloths?!" Wes called over his shoulder as he ran down the hill towards the water. "Let's go, pick up the pace, or we're going to miss the boat!"

"I'm not as tall as you!" she scolded, running after them, now in last place.

Wes had asked one of his friends to take them punting.

Beth had already been punting once that summer when the Yale in London group had traveled to Cambridge to have dinner with the Master of Magdalene, but Wes had prevailed on her regardless; quickly explaining that his friend gave the best tours.

There would be plenty of lurid tales and flasks and swearing. "Everything you love, Liz!" he'd said.

She crossed the bridge, holding onto her bag as it bounced wildly, her things clanging inside.

She looked down over the bridge at the water. They were already inside. She put her head down and really made a run for it, deciding to feel the fun of it instead of worrying about catching up.

She never got to run anymore; even running to class was really a fast walk or jog. She was by no means a runner, but she missed *running*.

Running across a great big green lawn. Running down a hill. Running into the ocean. She resolved right then and there that she would do more of it.

She laughed as her pony tail fell to her shoulders and then fell completely. Her hair blew wildly in the wind, billowing out behind her. She'd just reached the edge, rounding the bridge and turning towards the water when she smacked into someone.

Hard.

She fell backwards, but the person she'd run into flung his arms out and caught her before she fell to the ground. In one quick move he placed her upright again.

He bent down to pick up her bag, shaking his wild light brown hair out of his face.

She looked gratefully into his blue eyes, made electric by the sun. "Thanks and sorry!" she said taking the bag from him.

Their fingers grazed each other in the exchange. It was a typical British summer, hot and humid, but a chill ran down her spine.

"Let's go!" Audre and Wes called together, bringing her attention back to the water.

She looked over at them gesturing impatiently from the boat.

"Well, see ya!" she smiled up into the handsome face of the man she'd just collided with.

He watched her go. "What's your name?" he called.

She half turned, with a mischievous smile she answered, "Just call me Fate!" She winked at him.

And then she got into the boat and drifted away.

Chapter 1: Only in Paris

The bitter-sweet dark chocolate and rich cream danced in Elizabeth's mouth as she savored the last bite of her chocolate éclair. Café de Flore in Saint-Germain-des-Prés was bustling with patrons and passers-by.

Across the boulevard elegant Parisians waltzed in and out of the sleek Armani store.

A woman in a skin tight, cap sleeve, white dress exits a black car across the street. Her oversized black sunglasses, red lips, perfectly coiffed hair, and silky Birkin bag exude purpose.

She talks on her cell phone and scans the street, clearly meeting someone. Elizabeth guesses it's a man.

She could be there for herself, but then she probably would have gone in directly. Perhaps she was a personal shopper or an attentive wife or girlfriend, or even a mistress.

A second later an expensive looking man emerges from a second car. They kiss on both cheeks and go through the glass doors.

It was one of Elizabeth's favorite things: people watching. And there was no better city for it than Paris. There were always interesting scenes unfolding, examples of life happening, micro-stories in the making.

Her photography brain rarely shut off.

Mostly, she recorded the scenes in her head. Only rarely was she compelled by a landscape to take out the camera. It had to be a very compelling image indeed to brave the looks of contempt and displeasure from her fellow patrons.

A camera was the number one identifier of the most despised label in Paris: *tourist*. Regardless of whether the equipment was professional grade.

Even with her camera bag at her feet she felt self-conscious; she knew that eventually she would get over it and acclimate to the sometimes judgmental Parisian culture.

It was the mark of a true Parisian: the ability to wear simple black with all the swagger of a movie star and to strut down the sidewalks with an *I don't give a damn* attitude.

Elizabeth often thought about the difference in cultures she had encountered in the five months she'd been away from San Francisco.

Parisians were the most perplexing by far. They could be friendly when they wanted, rude when it suited them, and downright mean if prompted. Nice and naive were the attributes most often met with the rude and the mean.

It wasn't that the French went out of their way to be nasty, it was that they really understood life. Understood that there was really no point—or time—for bullshit.

The world could learn a lot from them, she thought. Their *joie de vivre*, effortless elegance, discerning tastes and colorful opinions made them a fascinating people. She had enjoyed rediscovering this about them.

Next to the Armani store was the Emporio Armani Caffè. A gleaming black box with crystal clear windows in the center, like a chocolate macaron with a clear jelly filling.

The patrons were posh and wore black and white, matching the decor. Beth watched the two couples sitting at small tables by the windows. They were having completely different days.

A blonde in a black mini dress leaned back in her chair, crossing her arms and legs simultaneously. The man with flecks of gray in his hair, and an impeccable suit sat opposite her.

He was in his mid-forties while she was in her mid-twenties. She could tell they were both French from the way their lips moved, the way their tongues wrapped around the words.

The blonde glared daggers at him as he leaned forward using his hands to explain something vitally important, his ring caught the light. It wasn't difficult to guess what their relationship might be.

For a moment Elizabeth envisioned the wife. Where was she on this bright balmy Tuesday afternoon? And how soon after they'd promised forever had it stopped being enough?

Behind the couple arguing sat a brunette in a black shirt and white skirt. She was leaning forward her hands both enveloped by the man sitting opposite her. They were in their late twenties or early thirties—completely oblivious to the two people having a row just inches behind them. With each sentence, each laugh they drew closer until finally their lips met and they kissed openly with abandon.

She wanted to laugh at the contrast between the two sets. Only in Paris. Only in Paris could people argue with such passionate abandon in public and kiss so wildly in such close proximity.

The kissing partners made something in her chest ache for Connor, her beautiful Irishman. It had been two weeks since he'd handed her a box with a big crystal on a simple chain.

To others it was an inexpensive bauble, to Connor it was one of his most prized possessions. It was part of an irreplaceable memory, a clear manifestation of his mother's love for him. To Beth it was priceless.

She'd run out of the Natural History Museum in London after winning Wildlife Photographer of the Year. Taking the steps of the main entrance in her five-inch heels and running past the gathered crowd until she'd finally caught up with him.

Finally given in to her feelings.

Finally given in to the gorgeous Irishman with the blue eyes, light brown hair and green Celtic Cross on his arm; whom she'd unexpectedly seen naked on that very first day.

He kissed her outside the museum like it was the final scene of some Hollywood movie. A fairytale ending—except it wasn't an ending—it was their beginning.

They'd spent the next week and a half in bed. Or curled up on the couch together. Or wrapped around each other in Rose Square.

They rarely ventured out beyond a few instances in Belgravia and Hyde Park, always hand in hand.

One notable exception had been when Connor had surprised her with a private tour of the Harry Potter Studio outside of London. He bribed someone to let them have free rein of the place after it had closed to the public and the staff had gone.

She smiled, looking down at the green Café de Flore table as she remembered.

"Mon Amour," a young voice brought her back to the present. "J'ai besoin de toi. S'il te plaît!" A young man, barely out of his teens sped past the crowded tables under the white awning and green lettering of the café on the corner of the famous Boulevard Saint-Germain. "No, no, noo . . ." he said into his phone before disappearing down the street.

There was nothing like June in Paris. It was only their third day in the city together, but already the alternating cool breezes and thick humidity—the sun and the flowers—had a strange effect.

It was spring and summer and love and sex, the air was heavy with it. Passionate scenes flooded the streets, the parks, the open spaces. Emotions were running high.

Or maybe that was just Paris.

Her phone buzzed against the table.

Be there in three, Luv. —Connor

A strange little jolt ran through her. She still wasn't used to it. Used to being in a relationship full of love and passion and everything you hear about in songs. Just the thought of him, could put her in a euphoric, up in the clouds sort of state.

She shook her head clear and turned around to make eye contact with the waiter, "L'addition, s'il vous plaît." She motioned with her hand.

He walked over to her and set the bill down on the table. "Merci, Mademoiselle," he said and walked off.

She looked back at her phone, scrolling through her email while she waited for Connor.

After she'd decided not to go back to San Francisco she had created a new email account which, initially, only Mr. Lewis the private investigator she'd hired to find Matthieu, had access to.

But as she slowly reconnected with others—Audre, Loryn, Wes, and her friends back in Ireland of course, it had started to fill up again. Between her friends, new and old, and unexpectedly winning a major photography award, she was just starting to get used to having to check it again.

How much had changed in six months. Her inbox used to be filled with notes on cases and conferences and depositions. It used to be the perfect picture of all that could go wrong in a relationship.

Two people doing everything in their power to extract themselves from one another. The sad remnants of a life once shared, reduced to boxes filled with legal documents, and gigabytes on a computer.

Now her inbox contained email updates from people who cared about her, pictures of happiness, and in the last two weeks she'd also started to get emails from completely unexpected places.

The award had come with international exposure and she'd been contacted by National Geographic, a handful of travel magazines, and two galleries—one in London, the other in New York—that expressed an interest in showing her work.

On one level it was thrilling, and on another it was unbelievable.

Her relationship with Connor was so beyond anything she could have expected that the photography offers seemed unreal. It was just too much good all at once—like a waking dream.

After their reunion outside the museum, they'd experienced a good week and a half of uninterrupted bliss when they couldn't stand to be apart from each other. It was the type of reunion where both parties felt the strong pull to keep within reaching distance of each other.

It was less a desire and more of an aching need—to feel him next to her—to feel her breathing against him.

They were definitely out of Fantasyland—their relationship was more real than anything she'd ever experienced before, but some small part of her still thought it was too good to be true.

She wasn't the doom and gloom type, not even during her lost decade. But the lawyering life she'd left behind and the train-wreck marriages she'd been privy to during that time stayed with her—like ghosts.

It was impossible to fully divorce herself from them. After all, it had only been six months and she'd witnessed so many ways that relationships could fall apart.

Love could and often did, *end*.

She heard him before she saw him. Her lips twitched up involuntarily at his deep Irish cadences.

"Well, do we know anything yet?" Connor said.

There was something wrong with his voice, it was higher, more strained.

Her eyes found him just around the corner of the café. He had stopped to talk to someone on his cell phone. Facing the windows of the business next door, he had one hand on his hip.

"Oh? What does Auguste say?" He waited for an answer.

"Yeah I know Nadine, but we've got to get this sorted. Does he think it's a prank? Some nutter—" He stopped talking to listen to the person on the other line.

Beth leaned forward arching her neck so she could see him as he took a few steps away from the café. She knew that he probably had no idea she could hear him.

What was happening?

She'd seen Connor at his most agitated and this wasn't it.

But still. There was something wrong.

Since moving to the most romantic city in the world three days ago, they'd barely seen each other. He'd been off dealing with his auction house, *Bannon's*. It had already experienced a couple of delays and she knew he was getting frustrated with the project.

Looking back on how much time he'd spent away from his work to be with her over the last few months, it was astounding the auction house was going forward at all.

She felt the complement in it . . . and his devotion to her.

She felt his absence acutely, but she filled her days easily. It was such a walkable city and Beth was grateful to find that the time flew by.

She was in Paris with money and time to spare, and a camera in her hands—it was a different kind of bliss all on its own. But like most people in love, she felt that constant pull, that constant need to be near him.

She shook her head, realizing that she'd stopped listening, distracted by her own thoughts.

"Fine, just contact the authorities in any case . . . yeah, I'm sure." He let out all of the air in his lungs in a huff, "And get me that list of personnel. There are certain things that I'm not willing to risk."

He nodded silently into the phone and then ended the call, slipping the phone into the pocket of his slacks. He stood there for a moment with his hands on his hips staring into the window down the street.

He looked frustrated . . . and more than a little concerned.

She was just about to get up and go to him, when someone rammed into her chair from behind, shaking the table.

"Pardon!" A female voice said, her tone was anything but apologetic, it went beyond the typical French rudeness— the voice was full of something Beth would have labeled loathing if she didn't know any better.

Beth stared at the back of the woman's spiky black head. She weaved her way through the narrow tables and crossed the street just as another car stopped in front of the Armani store and blasted Kelly Joyce's *Vivre La Vie*.

"Lara!" Connor called from several feet away, refocusing her attention. His face split into his Christmas morning grin. The big chords of Joyce's song seemed to grow louder as he approached—almost in slow motion—his wavy hair caught the breeze, like a model on a runway.

Stunned by his entrance, she didn't have time to get up and greet him before he sat down in the chair next to hers. He leaned over, bringing her into his arms, the light fabric of his expensive black blazer felt cool under her fingers.

Something in her chest relaxed as he held her. She didn't want him to let go. He withdrew slightly, but only so he could capture her lips with his. It was a kiss fraught with longing and tension, desperation and relief, love and lust.

14

Normally she would have shied away from such an intense public display, but here in Paris . . . in his arms, it felt like the most natural thing in the world.

After five seconds or five minutes, he let go to rest his forehead against hers.

"Hi," he breathed. Something in his chest relaxed when he'd kissed her.

She smiled dreamily and then the phone conversation pierced her lust-filled haze. Her eyebrows drew together, "What was that about? On the phone just now, what's happening?"

Connor released her, taking her right hand in both of his and resting it on his lap. He looked down at their fingers, and shook his head. "It's nothing to worry about, just something at the auction house." He looked into her eyes trying but failing to put her at ease.

She tilted her head, "What are you playing at Bannon? Something is obviously wrong; you're supposed to tell me the absolute truth and not keep anything from me, remember? That's how this works." She used her freehand to motion between them.

He brought his shoulders half way up to his ears, and squeezed her hand, "It's nothing, really. Just some odd phone calls, and there may have been a security breach. We aren't sure because nothing appears to have been taken."

"That's . . . strange? Do you have anything of value in the space yet? I thought you were keeping everything off-site until the remodel is finished."

"We are, that's why it's nothing to worry about. But, I am making sure we report the calls and our suspicions so that there's a paper trail, in case it turns out to be more serious."

He squeezed her hand again. "See, Luv? Nothing to worry about, it's all under control."

She raised an eyebrow. "You sounded pretty agitated."

He shrugged, "You heard that, did you?"

She nodded.

"Well, I find I have less patience for this new venture as the days get on. It doesn't usually feel like work . . . but it's . . . *difficult*, to be away from you."

His eyes found the still kissing couple across the street just then. The quarreling twosome had already gone.

"I find myself dealing with these troubling bits differently. It's become more of a nuisance to set up this particular house."

He sat back in his chair and looked at her. "And that all started when I met you." He touched the tip of her nose with his index finger.

"Is that your way of saying you missed me?"

"Yes, Lara. I definitely missed you." Paris seemed to electrify his ice blue eyes more than usual. They melted her insides.

He looked around, taking in the surroundings, "Why are you at Café de Flore? It's a bit touristy for you, isn't it? Oh wait, let me guess you're a Hemingway fan."

"Eh, he's all right, I'm here for Simone de Beauvoir and Chagall, of course. And it was convenient, I was taking

16

pictures of the church up the block." She pointed up the street defensively.

The touristy spots in Paris were all worth seeing in their own right. The cafés, the galleries and museums, the landmarks—they were beautiful and historic and worth seeing again and again.

But there was something about this visit to Paris. She wanted to be a part of the city. It would take a lot more than three days to make her feel like a Parisian, but at the very least she wanted to not be seen as a tourist.

Sensing this desire or perhaps reading the thoughts as they crossed her face, he held up his free hand, "My mistake."

He turned his attention to the street signs, orienting himself. "Well, as it happens, this is an excellent spot. We don't even have to take the car. Let's just take a stroll."

He motioned to a black town car across the street. Bertrand nodded and pulled into traffic.

Understanding dawned, her eyes lit up, "Is it really happening?"

He nodded with a big smile.

She extracted her hand from his and laced her fingers together under her chin like he'd just given her a present. "Really?"

Her amusement made him laugh.

Since they had arrived on Sunday they'd called the Ritz home, because Connor's apartment renovations had fallen behind schedule.

She'd left the hotel with her bags packed and ready to go this morning, but all the fashionable French delays had taught her to be cautiously optimistic.

"Why do you look so surprised? I told you it was happening today. I wasn't coddin' you."

"I know, but part of me didn't think it would be ready."

His mouth dropped in mock shock, "When have I ever lied to you?"

Beth narrowed her eyes. He'd never technically lied to her, but he'd certainly left a whole host of details out at times.

"Okay, okay." He held up both of his hands defensively now. "Too soon?" he said referring to the tabloid showing him kissing a supermodel in this very city while she was in London.

It had all been a ploy to get her attention. To coax out her feelings for him. And it had backfired royally. Driving her to seek out a romance with her good friend Wes Cartwright.

"Come on, up you get," he said standing and reaching for her hand.

Elizabeth left the money and maneuvered herself between the narrow tables to get to him. They walked hand-in-hand up Boulevard Saint-Germain, passing the green awning of another famous café frequented by Hemingway and de Beauvoir and Picasso, Les Deux Magots.

They crossed the street to Rue Bonaparte, passing Cartier and Swarovski. When they passed Cartier, Connor jokingly suggested they go in. There was a strange glint in his eye which caused a small pit to form in her stomach.

She wouldn't notice it until later.

Rue Bonaparte was a small one-way street filled with quaint but expensive shops and cafés on the first floor of classic Parisian residential buildings.

There were elegant watch shops, specialty sports stores, and an upscale pharmacy. There was a gallery with a poster of a man in his sixties wearing a black shirt, arms crossed standing in a space with wooden floors; paintings and sculptures peppered the background. The poster had only one word: "Alexandre" followed by a date and a time.

There were ads for a Rolex in the windows of the store next door, and ads for decadent face creams you would normally find at Sephora in the States, in the windows of the pharmacy across the street.

"So how's Bannon's coming, then?" she asked him as they continued down Rue Bonaparte.

"Oh, I dunno. Alright, I suppose. Auguste has his hands full with security. Nadine and Roger seem to have the paintings and novelty collections well in hand. And the space is nearly finished. . . ."

He poked her in the ribs playfully, "But this used to be more fun. Now I'd rather spend all my time with you. The me I was a year ago would take the mickey out of the me that is standing here with you."

He stopped. "Did that make any sense at'all?"

"No," she smiled and wrapped an arm around his waist. "And *yes*."

They passed the rich green exterior and gold lettering of À la Mère de Famille, the dessert shop that claimed to be the oldest chocolatier in Paris, dating back to the eighteenth century. Elizabeth stopped to look at the colorful, chocolaty confections through the glass.

He reached for the gold handle on the green door. "We can go in. Come on."

She stopped him. "No, no, no. I want to see the apartment. You can get me chocolate later." She grinned up at him.

He narrowed his eyes teasingly, "Well good, I will. If anything just to hear your foodgasm sounds. That's a talent all on its own—the way you enjoy your sweets." He tried to tickle her, she swatted him away.

Across the square from a church hidden behind a set of very old trees, there was a long line of connected tents set up on the sidewalk. A white sign with big bold red letters announced: "Antiquaires".

Connor's stride slowed as he took in the sign. She could feel the pull for him to go and look through the wares.

She tugged on his arm, "We can go." She moved to cross the street.

He didn't budge, "No, no, no," he smiled down at her. "I really want to show you the apartment."

They stared at each for a moment, like lovesick teenagers. Her heart fluttered. What was happening? How did people in love *function*?

When they reached Rue de Vaugirard, and the big imposing black metal fence that ran along the opposite side of the street, enclosing the Luxembourg Palace and Gardens, they turned left.

Posters of the Tudors hung on the museum walls facing the street. One was a giant billboard-like image of Henry VIII in a power stance with the words, "Les Tudors" announcing an exhibit currently running at the Luxembourg Museum.

She turned her attention back to the street. "How much farther?"

"It's just up here." He stopped a couple of blocks past the corner of Rue Bonaparte and Rue de Vaugirard. "Up there." He pointed to the top floor of a very Parisian building.

It stood almost two floors above all the others around it. It was classic Paris and an anomaly at the same time. Its features were more striking, more pronounced, but the floors were all level with the lines of its neighbors.

She wondered how it had escaped the Haussmann Renovations of the nineteenth century that imposed height and floor restrictions and were responsible for so much of what people considered Parisian architecture.

She looked up shielding her eyes from the sun with her hand "How many stories is it?"

"Ten. Not including the ground floor, o' course."

She turned to him with some humor in her voice, "Please tell me there's an elevator."

He pulled her in front of him, his arms wrapped around her waist. "Oh there's a lift." He kissed her cheek and then her jaw and then her neck until she giggled.

"Come on," he said grabbing her hands and turning into a road too small for cars. It was more like a really quaint alley with classic black Paris lamps attached to the buildings, the bottom floors all painted in red, blue or green according to the different shops.

Elizabeth found the small blue sign naming it Rue Servandoni.

Connor stopped a few feet into the alley, at a bright red front door.

She wanted to laugh at the continuity. This was the third red front door she'd had since leaving San Francisco at the beginning of February.

He took out his keys and ushered her through.

Chapter 2: Glimmering Chandeliers

"Ready, Lara?" Connor took her hand, "Close your eyes."

They'd just taken the elevator to the top floor.

"No, just show me already!" she refused. Her lips twitched up as she registered the mischief in his eyes. His lips set in a line as he out-waited her.

"Ugh, fine," she relented.

She shut her eyes and let herself be led through the front door of the apartment. Connor took her a few steps inside, letting the door close behind them.

"Okay, Miss Lara," Connor instructed.

She opened her eyes and found herself in a formal foyer. The floors were a beautiful rich stained bamboo, Connor had insisted the renovations be eco-friendly wherever possible.

On the wall to her right was a large mirror. The frame was made out of a shiny silver-like metal with an intricate Celtic knot design. Underneath was a long console table.

Above was a crystal chandelier that lit the space surprisingly well. There were six small doors along the left wall which turned out to be a spacious closet.

Without looking back at Connor she stepped beyond the foyer and into what turned out to be the big open living area, lit by five massive windows.

It took her breath away.

"Welcome home," Connor said with no small amount of pleasure.

She let her feet propel her forward, completely ignoring him, which she rightly supposed made him very happy.

That was his measure for how taken she was by something—when her feet compelled her automatically forward.

She went first to the small sitting area directly opposite the foyer, it was a reading nook of sorts. Two large bookcases stood from floor to ceiling with two high-back tufted armchairs, one black, one white, and a small wooden coffee table between.

She went next to the large black tufted leather sectional which reminded her very much of one she'd seen at Castle Bannon. Her fingers trailed the smooth leather as she walked around it, moving next to the large white French country couch that could've been the twin of the one at the cottage at Lough Rhiannon.

Three striking pieces of art hung on the walls between the long ivory draped windows. A Chagall, a sketch of a Canova, and a Degas.

She walked to the glass but didn't get close enough to see the full view. She'd save that for later. All she could tell was that the living area faced Jardin du Luxembourg and Rue Vaugirard.

The kitchen took up a great deal of the far wall. She ran her fingers over the butcher block countertop, taking in the French farmhouse lighting fixture surrounded by thinner copper lights that hung from the ceiling like tear drops.

While she was looking up she noticed all of the wonderful, elegant crown molding that could only be found in the oldest apartments in Paris.

An open door next to the cabinets, beckoned. She thought it might be a pantry.

What she found instead was a long rectangular formal dining room. Twelve chairs sat comfortably around the large table, although it probably could have accommodated eighteen without difficulty. The space had a definite air of formality, but the table was more French farmhouse than elegant dining room; the piece was polished, long and thick.

The chairs were elegantly chic, clearly a matching set, but all of them had different details. The rich upholstery ranged in color from ivory to black to royal blue and bright green. The backs were round with little individual woodcarvings at the top of each.

A Celtic knot, the Eiffel tower, the London bridge, an outline of the Cliffs of Moher, the Golden Gate Bridge, a lighthouse, the setting sun—maybe it was rising, she couldn't tell. Her fingers traced each carving in turn moving around the table until she noticed a closed door.

Apparently, the next long rectangular space was a library with floor to ceiling shelves. A rich green expensive looking rug covered the wood floors. There were two high-back tufted armchairs, twins of the ones in the reading nook.

The other furniture in the room included a smaller black leather couch, a longish table with three desk lamps, and a rolling ladder on each wall.

Elizabeth followed the doors.

The next one went in the opposite direction of the Luxembourg Gardens. It revealed a massive all-purpose room. Landlocked with no windows, it was darker than the other rooms, but only slightly. Light still managed to get through.

Her eyes traced the brightness back to its source—a series of skylights dispersed light evenly throughout the eclectic area.

Two rows of plush leather theatre seats faced a wall on one end. A sudden noise and a dramatic change in light made her aware of Connor for the first time.

She turned to find him near the door she'd just come through, his finger on a button that seemed to cover the skylights and lower a massive screen at the same time.

Elizabeth laughed, "A theatre? Really?"

"What'd you expect? I gutted the place. Designed it from top to bottom, o' course I was going to add a theatre. We needed a space to watch the rest of the John Hughes classics I've missed."

She laughed, remembering their movie marathons in the theatre at Castle Bannon.

"And see here," he walked to the corner furthest away from the screen where a series of shelves framed the two walls next to a desk and an antique wood armoire.

"You can keep your photography equipment here or you can use one of the bedrooms that has better light if you prefer. We have the space to do what we fancy."

She bit her lip looking up into his blue eyes, the tenderness there, the desire to please was not lost on her.

There were things to say . . . but the rest of the apartment beckoned.

She opened the door adjacent to the theatre screen, poking her head into a bedroom that faced the street. A large four-poster, a night stand, a chandelier, and a white mantelpiece, adorned the space.

It was simple and elegant, just the way she would've done it. She walked in the opposite direction, towards what turned out to be a long hallway.

The hallway was aligned like an enfilade; Beth could see straight back through to the foyer and beyond that, the front door to the apartment.

The last door across the hall was another bedroom, slightly bigger, but nearly identical to the one she'd just seen.

It faced a third street that was just as quaint as Rue Servandoni.

She walked out to the hall and back to the living area, finally looking back at Connor with her full attention. "Oh Connor, it's *gorgeous.*"

He crossed his arms and swayed in place, throwing her a look that said *there's more.*

Remembering the view she'd saved, she walked straight to the windows. As she drew nearer, she realized that they were actually doors that opened onto a balcony.

Turning the smooth handle, she stepped through to find a spectacular view of Palais du Luxembourg and Jardin du Luxembourg across the street.

The imposing wrought iron fence with gold tipped arrows that surrounded the Palace and Gardens was no match for the height of the apartment. She could see part of the museum, into the gardens, and even part of the Bassin.

She whipped around to face him, leaning back on the railing, "Your apartment is *bril*-liant," she nodded, eyes wide.

He stepped out onto the balcony with her, his expression muted. Narrowing his eyes, "*Our* apartment, Lara," he said pointedly.

She hadn't meant anything by it. It was his—just a fact, but she could hear the annoyance in his voice.

"*Your* apartment," she said again. "It's stunning, but Connor it's your apartment." Her voice was light and matter of fact, completely devoid of any bad connotation.

What was the big deal? She didn't love it any less. . . .

"It's wonderful!" she said with glee.

He pursed his lips and walked back inside, she followed.

She tried to lighten the mood, letting her genuine excitement for the place color her voice. "Which bedroom do we sleep in?"

He was still annoyed, but she could tell she'd successfully gotten him to switch gears. "Which bedroom would you *like* to sleep in?" He walked back into the living area, stopping at the long black sectional.

"Hmmm . . . I think I like the bedroom facing the gardens." She wiggled her eyebrows, "No question."

"*Do* you?" He turned away from her and put his hands in his pockets, walking towards a door she hadn't yet noticed. When he reached it, he angled half of his body towards her.

His eyes grew bright as he considered what to say next, "I have a better idea."

He turned the knob, "I think *this* space is more suited to us," he said, throwing the door open.

Elizabeth didn't know what to expect. Cautiously, like it was equally possible that a live lion or a giant cake lay beyond, she stepped inside.

There was a massive king-size dark wood four-poster with cream colored gauze-like drapes. Elegant Celtic knot carvings ran up the columns.

There was a sitting area with a French country chic loveseat and two white high-back armchairs that matched the others.

A gorgeous chandelier framed by an intricate circular molding made the room feel palatial.

The master sat on the corner. Two full walls of windows ushered in a barrage of light. Her feet carried her forward, her mouth dropped.

From the foot of the bed the view was a straight shot to none other than the Eiffel Tower. She could even see part of the green space at its foot, the Champs de Mars.

"Holy crap," she said under her breath. Connor snickered behind her. Her feet took her involuntarily to the balcony to see if it was an illusion.

It wasn't.

The balcony wrapped around to the other wall which had an even more splendid view of the Luxembourg Gardens.

This was Paris. Opulent . . . gorgeous . . . historic . . . *breathtaking.*

She closed her eyes still seeing the imprints of the images behind her lids and then opened them again to see if it was all still there.

She did it once more, her lips twitched up as some childhood like glee rose up inside of her. Before she could open them again Connor came up and wrapped his arms around her from behind.

"Do you like our apartment, Lara?" he whispered against her earlobe. She angled her head away to keep him from tickling her, and then opened her eyes again for one final confirmation.

Her mouth dropped, ready to say *your* apartment once more, but thought better of it. It would ruin the moment.

"I love it," she whispered instead, thinking it was simple and to the point. Never mind that technicality now.

She loosened his hands around her waist and laced them through her own.

She tapped at his hand playfully, "Okay, how far are we from everything?" Her voice was thick with excitement. She was rewarded when she felt him grin wide against her cheek.

"Well . . . we're a seventeen minute walk to Notre Dame, that way." He pointed to the left behind them. "Or five minutes by car. Twenty minutes to Musée Rodin, maybe ten by car. And we're a thirteen minute drive to La Tour Eiffel, I'd wager forty-five on foot. The walk from Café de Flore and the main area of Saint-German, just now was about ten minutes."

Elizabeth had a sudden urge to settle in, to walk barefoot around the entire apartment. The soft wood under her feet, a box of chocolates in one hand, a glass of wine in the other.

She turned in his arms and laced her fingers behind his neck. "We should go get our things from the Ritz."

He grinned, tightening his arms around her, "It's all here, check the closet."

She released her hands letting them fall down his arms and raised an eyebrow. There was *more*?

She pushed Connor backwards and maneuvered around him, reentering the master suite. There was a whole other wall she hadn't noticed.

One door led to an en suite with marble countertops, a double sink, a massive Jacuzzi tub with separate shower, and another shining crystal chandelier above. A green accent rug covered the sleek floor.

The other set of doors opened up into a massive closet where she found her luggage stacked in a neat pile in the middle of what could've been another bedroom entirely.

There was a door that went out onto the same balcony as the rest of the master suite, directly from the closet—a feature she'd never seen before.

Thinking she might want to change soon, she drew the long cream drapes shut and immediately got to work on settling in. She placed the massive suitcases and the other bags she'd acquired during her five month long trip, in front of her.

She sunk down to the floor, taking off her black wedges and folding her dark skinny jean-ed legs underneath her. She rolled up the sleeves of her delicate white blouse, her movements were decidedly determined.

Connor watched her, leaning against one of the door frames, arms crossed, "Well don't you look right at home." He beamed at her.

She didn't look up, "It's what you wanted, isn't it?" She started to unload the top layer of the big suitcase—boxes of shoes. She slid them against the back half of the closet, claiming that side as hers.

"I did that," he mused. "But you so rarely oblige me. I'm just a bit shell-shocked."

He bent down and mimicked her pose on the floor, looking quite strange indeed with his expensive blazer and nice slacks. His hair was perfectly coiffed out of his eyes. "Fancy some help?"

She knew what he looked like without taking her eyes from the suitcase—he looked delicious. "No thanks." She refused to catch his eyes or she would get sucked into the bottomless pool of blue.

"If you're not going to unpack your things maybe you could grab me a glass of wine?" She shooed him away with her hand.

He walked out of the closet laughing. "White or red?" he called behind him.

"You already know the answer to that, thank you!" she raised her voice so he would hear.

He was back a couple of minutes later, when she was nearly halfway through the unpacking. It would take her much longer to organize it all, but it was enough to have some of her clothing hanging neatly on the rack and her favorite boots stacked on top of the shoe boxes.

He handed her a glass of dry sauvignon blanc, it activated her taste buds all at once, making her cringe. Her palette acclimated after taking another sip. It was lovely. She could taste the peach and the pear; it had a nice long finish.

She'd taken a wine tasting course her senior of college. It was one of the most useful classes Yale offered.

Most of the time, she was quite adept at tasting all of the bits and pieces of a wine, but even when she couldn't taste anything remarkable in a glass, she'd learned and retained enough to throw out long meaningless descriptions.

It's got a smoky open, with hints of berry and undertones of earth, and a nice dry finish. When she'd been particularly bored at law fundraisers she'd made a game of stringing together random words and declaring them confidently.

The men around her would nod sagely and partially agree with her. *Yes, I agree with the open and earthy undertones, but I daresay I detect citrus and not berries.*

She smiled, remembering how she'd played that particular game once with a California Supreme Court Justice.

Connor stood over her drinking his glass, watching her closely.

After taking a few more sips, she reached up and handed her glass back to him. "Would you set it down in the kitchen or on the nightstand? I don't want the wine near the clothes."

Connor stilled, letting the silence grow between them.

Finally, she looked up at him, "What are you looking at?"

His lips twitched up, but he didn't quite make it to a smile. His eyes took on a new intensity, a feeling so pure it shot straight into her heart.

He was looking at her with such devotion, such passion that the blood rose to her face and spread throughout her body. "I love you, Lara."

Then his mood turned, he let the thick Irish accent back in, "You're a fine bit o' stuff, y'are." He narrowed his eyes, teasing.

She tilted her head waiting for an explanation.

He set the wine glasses down on the floor and came down to her eye level, "It means you're gorgeous, ma chérie." He leaned forward on his knuckles and kissed her lightly.

Elizabeth was about to wrap her arms around his neck and bring him down on her when he pulled away, standing up quickly.

She narrowed her eyes at his tease.

He knew exactly what he was doing.

He gave her a smug smile. "Welcome to your new home—" he stopped abruptly, looking at her.

She had opened her mouth to argue, but she wasn't sure what she should say.

They hadn't talked about this part yet. About what happened next; what happened after she found Matthieu, delivered Mags' message about Elsa . . . and maybe got to meet her father, once Brian was able to tell her more.

As amazing as the apartment was, her legal brain would never see it as part hers.

Maybe that would change?

Connor recognized all the thoughts as they crossed her face. His expression had changed from sheer happiness to one of deep concern, he folded his arms against his chest.

She could tell he was thinking through what to say next, but she wouldn't give him the opportunity. It wasn't time for this conversation and, as it stood, she would have no idea what to say.

Instead, she stood up, taking evasive maneuvers.

He straightened, clearly aware of her change in body language. She placed her hands on his forearms bringing them down to her waist. Reaching behind her, she pushed his wrists down so his palms were now firmly on her backside.

She could tell he was trying not to smile, but appreciative mischief showed in his eyes. She wrapped her arms around his neck and raised herself on her tiptoes to kiss him.

Initially they were featherlight, playful kisses, and then she forcibly took his lips. He responded instantly, flexing his fingers, kneading her, using his hands to press her against him.

In one lithe movement he lowered his hands until they were just beneath her buttocks. He flexed his biceps and lifted her to him, she wrapped her legs around his waist as he carried her out of the closet and over to the bed.

He carried her to the edge, then carefully lowered them both, never breaking the kiss. With a few quick moves he chucked his shoes aside.

Then he brought their bodies up so they were both kneeling on the bed. He unbuttoned her blouse slowly and let it fall down her shoulders, bringing his lips to her neck, to her collarbone, and then back up to her mouth.

He brought his hands down to her hips and pushed her up into a standing position, bringing his tongue down to her navel, kissing the flesh above her jeans. He unbuttoned her pants and wedged his hands inside, peeling them off of her until she could step out.

Standing there in just her undergarments, she placed her hands on the tops of his shoulders and hugged him.

He brought his head back to her stomach and then kissed lower until his mouth was directly over her sex, teasing her through the thin fabric of her underwear.

She let her head fall back with a moan that filled the silent space of their new bedroom. In that moment, it did feel like *theirs*.

Hearing the loaded sound coming from her chest, he quickly undid her bra, freeing her breasts and moving his tongue up to greet them.

After a few seconds, his hunger, his need for her, took over. With one arm, he grabbed her by the waist and threw her back onto the bed, sliding her underwear off as soon as she hit the mattress.

He extricated himself from his blazer throwing it to the floor and removed the rest of his clothing in record speed until he was hovering over her, supporting his weight with his hands placed on either side of her head.

His eyes roamed over her features, taking in her rosy cheeks, her beautiful green eyes, her full mouth.

Elizabeth registered the desire in his eyes, the devotion. She could almost see a lifetime of love there, in the sea of blue she'd come to know so well.

He kissed her slowly, keeping his eyes open. Watching her respond to him.

"Connor," she whispered against his lips.

He watched as her need for him deepened, then pushed his hips forward.

She closed her eyes and turned her head, arching her back.

Their bodies tangled together, in a symphony of movement. Doing as Parisians do, making love with reckless abandon and finding an earth-shattering release that made even the glimmering chandelier above quiver.

CHAPTER 3: ROSE SQUARE

Elizabeth drew small circles on Connor's bare chest.

They were lying naked together; Connor's arm wrapped around her shoulders, her head nestled in the crook of his shoulder.

With half open lids, "What are ya thinkin' about, Lara?"

She shook her head slightly, unable to do more than that. She felt a deep sense of belonging. Of contentment. But certain thoughts still danced around the edges of her subconscious.

Questions and expectations of meetings yet to come, were always on the horizon.

She continued to draw lazy circles over his skin.

He shifted his head so he could look at her, his voice thick with exhaustion, rough from pleasure, "What's the matter?" His fingertips stroked her arm.

"Nothing," she stretched up and leaned in to kiss his neck.

"Oh come now, Luv. I know you better than that. You're tracin' circles over and over in the same spot.

Somethin' is on your mind." He always sounded more Irish in bed.

"Are ya thinkin' about tomorrow?"

She didn't say anything. She hadn't been thinking about her meeting with Matthieu directly, but there was no denying that tomorrow was a very big day.

It was the end of the quest. The fulfillment of a dying wish, to find Matthieu, to meet him, and tell him about the daughter he never knew he had. To share the photos and stories that Mags had entrusted to her. Left for Matthieu on the SD card in letter four.

It wasn't like Beth not to answer. Connor stirred more decisively beside her, extracting his arm and using it to prop himself up, facing her. "It'll be fine, everything will be fine. It's what you've been waitin' for. And you know, you could look at it as, well sort of . . . " he hesitated. "Meeting family."

She looked at him then, "What? How?"

"Well from the letters we know that Matthieu was the love of Mags' life. The father to her only child. In a wee sense that kind of makes him your uncle?" He looked at her, unsure how she would take what he was saying, "Doesn't it? I know they were never married, but somehow it rings true."

She thought about that. She'd gotten so used to thinking that she was alone in the world, with no family left that the thought . . . she stopped, unable to consider it; to think of Matthieu as a pseudo-uncle. And she certainly didn't expect him to think of her as a niece.

She shook her head. "I don't know, I guess you could look at it that way . . . " she let the words flow from her mouth without attaching any tangible thought to them.

She looked up at the ceiling, focusing on the intricate twists and curls of the Parisian molding framing the chandelier.

"Has Brian told you anything else about your father?"

Ugh. There it was. The subject she'd really been avoiding—forcing it back behind some mental wall every time she thought of it.

Without looking at him, she shook her head. "No, not since two weeks ago when we talked in Rose Square."

A thin layer of fog had spread through the Square that chilly night in May when Brian, the executor of Mags' will and her longtime friend, had revealed himself and the true extent of her great-aunt's design.

And then he'd hit her with the biggest bombshell, telling her that he'd found her biological father. She'd sat there on the bench under the fifty foot London plane tree.

It was like being in a vacuum, all the air had been sucked away.

It took her some time to respond. For several minutes, or what seemed like several minutes, Beth just gaped at Brian. A handful of silent tears streamed down her face.

He'd looked at her with his Mr. Rogers like concern, reaching over to squeeze her arm gently.

"I apologize Elizabeth. It must seem like quite a barrage of life revelations. But I thought you would want to know. And unfortunately, I can't share the details with you yet. There are certain privacy issues involved and he hasn't been told about you."

His smile was tight, but kind.

With an imperceptible shake of her head, "How?" she said it so low she wasn't sure he could hear her.

But he answered, "Well as you know Mags had her suspicions even though Carolina never told her. I . . . found a close relative of the person she suspected and tested her against your DNA." He chose his words carefully.

"She did so voluntarily, but I'm afraid you did not. You could actually pursue legal action against me although I will tell you that it was Mags who found a way to get a hair sample from you. I just followed up," he shrugged.

Her eyes were wide, her expression blank. "*She?*" Elizabeth tried not to think too closely about what that meant. A sister . . . an aunt . . . a cousin?

He looked at his fingers, "Yes. For now that's all I can say. I'm sorry. I only received the results yesterday."

Her voice was still the ghost of a whisper. "Is that all you can tell me?"

"Yes, for now." He tried to sound reassuring. "It may be another month before I'm at liberty to tell you more. If I erred in telling you this . . . if I've . . . *revealed* this prematurely, without having all the facts for you, I'm very sorry."

He turned his palms up, "I made a judgment call."

She shook her head, "No, no—thank you. Thank you. . . . "

Their conversation had ended soon after. He'd hugged her goodbye and told her he would be in touch about her father and would liaise with Mr. Lewis to make arrangements for her to meet Matthieu in Paris.

He'd emailed on Saturday with the time and place. Musée Rodin at ten in the morning. *Tomorrow.*

Connor tapped her nose, bringing her back to the present, "Are you nervous?"

She grabbed his finger.

"A little," she admitted. But if she was being really honest with herself she was more nervous about seeing Brian again. About what he might have to say regarding her father.

All she knew was that he was alive. Beyond that she didn't know if he knew about her yet or if he wanted to see her. If she had any half siblings. Where he lived or how old he was. . . .

She shoved the questions and theories out of her mind.

She couldn't.

There was no point in going there since she didn't know when or if she would get those answers.

Always sensitive to her thoughts, Connor changed the subject, "So where did you end up today?"

She thought about his question, willing herself to take the out he'd given her, until finally she gave herself over to it. Just as he'd intended.

She told him about the small picturesque Jardin de la Nouvelle France, just off the Champs-Élysées. About lunch at Café du Petit Palais, a sanctuary garden with a pond and beautiful mosaic tables she'd found once some years ago after visiting the permanent art collection at the Petit Palais.

Finally coming to the photographs she'd taken of the thousand-year-old Benedictine Abbey of Saint-Germain-des-Prés.

Relieved she was starting to brighten, he continued, "And which pâtisserie did you find yourself at today?" This had the intended effect.

She'd happily recounted her travels, but now her eyes grew wide, a childlike glee elbowed its way to the front of her emotions, "*Jacques Genin,*" she said reverently.

He laughed, thoroughly enjoying how excited she could get about the sweets of Paris.

"Oh my God, I had a tarte au citron . . . the flavors were—*unbelievable*. I almost fell out of my chair, it was heaven."

She propped herself up on her elbow, all sense of drowsiness gone.

She continued even more animated than before, "And the chocolate éclairs—oh hell!" She arched her back and let her head fall backwards onto the pillow, melodramatically.

"Is that right." It wasn't a question. He eyed her curiously. Seeing her in a sugar inspired ecstasy roused him. He wanted to inspire another look of pleasure, to drive her to another sort of heaven.

Elizabeth didn't miss the change. He was looking at her like she was the dessert to eat. She could see it all there, in his eyes.

"Come here mon sucre d'orge. I'd like to take a bite out of you." He kissed her shoulder.

She looked at him, but angled her body away, still lost in the thoughts of all the pastry goodness she'd consumed that day. She placed her hands on his chest, "Already?"

He found his way to her neck anyway. "Well if you prefer," he licked the hollow between her collarbone and her shoulder. "We could move this party to the living area and re-create our snogging session from the Gryffindor Common Room when I took you to Hogwarts."

He said the last part in his British accent while wiggling his eyebrows suggestively.

"Hmmm . . . tempting," she considered.

She kissed him lightly and then smiled. Pulling away so she could see his face, "But you know . . . I think I'd rather we re-create what we did in Umbridge's Office. . . ." she whispered with a wicked grin.

His eyes met her mischief. "Ohhh, feeling bad are we?" He moved back to her neck. He was happy to oblige.

She pulled away laughing, but he didn't let her get far.

He wrapped his arms around her until she was flush against him, skin on skin.

Their bodies came together, their passions mounting quickly as the heat engulfed them for a second time.

CHAPTER 4: MATTHIEU

The significance of the day left her feeling a little naked—exposed. Like the very first day of school.

Connor had tried to keep her preoccupied, to take her mind off of the coming meeting, but at some point it had stopped working. She'd tossed and turned in his arms all night, until finally getting up at dawn.

She arrived at Musée Rodin at nine-thirty in the morning, thirty minutes before it opened, wearing a white cotton dress, black flats, and Mags' secret. Ever prepared, letters four and six were carefully tucked away in her shoulder bag for referencing.

Her heart thumped loudly in her ears as she approached the museum entrance.

Brian was already there dressed in a collared shirt and slacks, talking pleasantly on his cell phone. He noticed her right away and ended the call. "Elizabeth, how wonderful to see you again."

He greeted her with a hug, slipping the phone into his pocket. "Matthieu is already inside, would you like to go in?"

She looked back at her phone to make sure she had the time right. "I didn't think the museum opened for another half an hour . . . ?"

"It doesn't," he shrugged. "Matthieu is good friends with the staff. He comes here often. He's at *Le Penseur* now."

The main gate to Musée Rodin was a giant stone arch with massive doors.

Brian leaned on the main door until there was a gap large enough for them to step inside. They walked through the courtyard, bypassing the ticket booth, and into the main gardens.

All around them, birds chirped happily in the trees. Elizabeth's steps were punctuated by the crunching gravel underfoot. It was a strange sort of rhythmic soundtrack to her thoughts.

Her nerves began to rise up, either because she was about to meet the love of Mags' life or because she was about to ask Brian something—and she wasn't sure she wanted to know the answer.

They walked up the footpath through the shrubs and perfectly coiffed hedges that reminded her of giant green beautyblenders.

She crossed her arms and looked down at her feet as she considered how to ask, suddenly feeling like an awkward teenager, "Brian is there anything to tell on . . . *that* front?"

He looked at her sideways, giving her a kind smile. He knew what she was asking. "Yes Elizabeth, there's a great deal to tell."

He paused considering how best to explain.

The crunching gravel became all she could hear.

He stopped abruptly, making her turn. "But it isn't for me to tell. That being said, I believe you will soon know everything."

His soothing Mr. Rogers tone went a very long way to calm her nerves both on the subject of her father and for the experience she was about to have. She nodded and smiled at him gratefully. His knowing eyes acknowledged it all as they began walking again.

They hadn't gone far into the gardens, but it felt like a twenty minute walk to Beth instead of a two minute stroll.

They passed several sculptures, but she only had eyes for one. Auguste Rodin's most famous work stood near the front of the gardens, behind the museum.

She'd come here several times before and her feet knew the way. Without realizing it, she started walking faster than Brian and made a beeline for the flowers which sat parallel to the sculpture and provided one of the best views from a distance.

Her feet came to a stop in front of a bundle of yellow roses. She saw a man with gray hair and a dark brown blazer, his hands clasped behind his back. He stood at the foot of the piece, perfectly still.

She turned back to Brian who had just caught up.

"Go," he said, motioning with his head. "I'm going to take a stroll. It's such a treat to be alone here without other visitors."

He took a deep breath of fresh morning air, reminding her to do the same, and gave her a reassuring smile. "We'll all rendezvous after you've spoken."

She bit her lip from the inside and nodded. Turning back to the man she had sought for so long and the sculpture she knew so well, she went around the roses and found one of the diagonal paths that would take her where she needed to go.

There was no one nearby, not even the staff. Only the birds in the trees, her heartbeat, and the crunching gravel underfoot kept her company as she approached the man whom Magdalen had loved.

Finally.

His head tilted imperceptibly as she approached, but he remained at the base of the statue.

Someone else might have cleared their throat to get him to turn around so introductions could be made. But Elizabeth was guided by something outside of herself.

Instead, she took a few, slow steps until she was standing next to him. She planted her feet and looked up at *Le Penseur*. She'd stood on that very spot many times over the last seventeen years. It was one of her favorite places in Paris.

The bronze figure on its stone plinth always made her hair stand on end. Made her think about life and love and fate and the choices that had brought her to that very moment.

Matthieu spoke softly, careful not to disturb their shared reverie, "Isn't it marvelous." It wasn't a question. His voice scarcely had any trace of a French accent, in fact he sounded almost British. Almost.

She nodded. "Yes," she answered in that same soft tone.

For several moments they stood there, shoulder to shoulder, looking up.

When Elizabeth was through, she turned to the simple wooden bench lodged between two of the fifteen-foot-tall green beautyblenders, directly opposite the sculpture.

A couple of minutes later, Matthieu joined her.

She felt instantly at ease with him. There was something about the way he carried himself, the way he walked with the breeze, instead of against it. They'd scarcely said anything to each other but she could sense that he was a gentle soul.

She understood why Mags would have been drawn to him. He would've been a cool reprieve from her passionate fire. A place of repose, a home.

He angled his body towards her, "My Dear." He held out a hand and took hers in both of his, pulling her forward and giving her a very French, three cheek kiss.

She wanted to say *it's lovely to meet you* or *I'm so happy to finally know you*, but all she could do was smile and nod, letting her eyes express all that she could not say.

He nodded still holding her hand, understanding. He smiled kindly at her and then looked back at Rodin's work.

She looked back to the sculpture again too, letting her eyes take in the masterpiece from a distance as she thought of the words that would allow her to begin.

And then, as she searched for the right way, she suddenly realized that she hadn't thought about the beginning. She'd kept Mags' story about Elsa, her secret, in some distant part of her brain, thinking that when the time came, she'd be able to form the facts into a story that would make sense to her audience. Like an opening statement . . . or a closing argument.

Her stomach dropped as she realized, for the first time, that what she had to say to Matthieu would cost him great pain. She looked down at her hands, ashamed of how selfish she had been.

All that time of searching—at her great-aunt's request—and she'd never once thought about how difficult it would be for him to learn that he'd had a daughter? That she had died before he could know her?

And that Mags had kept that secret from him for more than fifty years?!

Her stomach made it all the way to her feet. How involved she'd been with her own drama. Her grief, her regret, it was all about her. And now she would have to sit and compose herself well enough to enlighten this gentle eighty-two-year-old man. To break his heart.

She took a deep breath, cleared her throat, and summoned the courage to do what she had been sent to do. "Monsieur Fleury," she began, trying and succeeding to sound composed. "How much did Brian tell you about why I'm here?"

His eyes crinkled. "Please Lizzie, it's Matthieu. May I call you Lizzie? It's the only name I've ever known for you."

His knowing Mags' moniker for her, felt strange, but reassuring. "You knew about me? You knew my name?"

"Oui, bien sûr!" He slipped into the French for *of course*.

He looked at her now, assessing the situation. "What did she tell you about our love affair?"

She looked back at the statue, "Only that you met in Verneuil-sur-Avre when you were twenty-six and she thirty-three. That you spent the summer with her there when she owned the pâtisserie. And then most weekends through that fall into the holidays."

He nodded, "Yes." He paused. "Did she tell you anything else?"

Without looking at him she continued, "You came together three more times in person over the course of your life times." Her voice wavered. It struck her how very sad their love story was.

He sighed beside her. "No sorrow, my Dear. Lena was the love of my life."

Elizabeth turned back to him.

His eyes crinkled, "And we *loved*." His words were wise, but his voice shook with the last word.

"And even though I hadn't laid eyes on her in twenty years, we've been writing to each other every week since the last time we saw each other here in Paris."

"And that's when she called me Lizzie? In the letters?" she asked, thinking about how he'd called Mags, Lena.

In Spanish, an 'a' was often added, so that it was pronounced Magdalena. She found it strangely thrilling that Mags had been known to others by different names.

The way she was Lizzie to only Magdalen and Matthieu, Beth to some, Liz to others, and Lara only to Connor.

He nodded. Of course they had been writing to each other for decades. After all, Mags had known exactly where to find him. Brian had said so on that misty night in Rose Square. She had wanted her to go out and find her life first . . . and *then* find Matthieu.

She looked at his hands, now clasped in his lap. They were crinkly and weathered, but soft looking.

The time was now. "There was . . . a reason she sent me to you," Elizabeth started.

He angled himself towards her again. "Yes, Brian said you had a message for me from my beloved."

Elizabeth swallowed, "Yes, she sent me to tell you something. To tell you about *someone.*"

She took a deep breath, there was nothing to do but say it, "Matthieu, I'm sorry to tell you this but . . . when you left to finish grad school and she left for Spain . . . Mags was pregnant. She found out a couple of months after leaving

France. She said that you had no way of getting in touch with each other. . . ."

He looked down at his hands lacing them together.

She continued trying to get through it quickly, but gently, "You had a daughter together. Her name was Elsa, but . . . she died when she was very young, just eight, in an accident. They were still living in Spain."

She said the next part in a rush, determined to get through the rest of it and give him all the information she had to give, "Mags didn't know how to tell you. She grieved for a very long time. And then when she saw you she said in her letter that she took such comfort in seeing you again that she needed you and so she didn't tell you because she *couldn't* tell you.

"The next two times you came together, she had different reasons for not telling you—I have the letter, you can read what she said. But, she also left you a video that she recorded on a memory card. It's for you, I haven't watched it, but I think you'll find some answers there.

"I'm very sorry to tell you all of this. All I can say on behalf of my aunt is that I'm sure she never meant to hurt you. She loved Elsa very much. They had a lovely life together—short, but wonderful . . . if that's any consolation."

She finished speaking, and found that she'd used all of the oxygen in her lungs. She took a deep breath, careful not to sound like she was gasping for air.

She let the revelation sit between them, giving it space to breathe.

Then she searched his hazel eyes. What she saw there surprised her. He didn't look heartbroken or shocked or even sad. He looked resigned and a little . . . *happy?*

He crossed his arms over his chest and smiled. It wasn't a happy smile or a sad one, but the smile of a man who'd known great loss and great joy. Who knew that sometimes smiling was all that could be done.

"Yes, I knew about Elsa. I went looking for my beloved Lena about seven years later. I had finished my degree and put in my time as a lowly professor.

"It was a six-month search, but I finally found her in a little village outside of Málaga. I saw her sitting on a bench in a park—she loved sitting on park benches—liked to watch the people go by.

"I was about to rush over when a little girl came bouncing up to her. The girl threw her arms around her neck and called her *mamá*. I was stunned. I thought perhaps she had found another and married. Magdalen gave Elsa some money to get an ice cream at the vendor just a few feet away.

"I approached the little girl and asked her if that woman was her mother. When she looked up at me I almost fainted."

He turned to Beth again, with a proud grin. "She had my eyes and my smile."

Beth returned his expression.

He continued the story, "I asked her for her name and where her father was. And the little girl said that he was a

56

professor in France, and that she'd never met him, but she hoped to one day.

"I asked her if her mother had a husband and she said no as the vendor handed her the ice cream. She took the treat and skipped away without a second thought and I was at a loss for what to do next.

"I found a big oak tree and watched them playing in the park together for an hour. I resolved right then and there to go find a prestigious post somewhere and come back in a few months. I would propose to her again and show her what I had to offer.

"When I returned nine months later with an excellent house to my name and a secure faculty position in London, I found that she had already left Spain. I spoke with a neighbor who told me about the accident."

His voice dropped to a whisper, "I was three months too late."

His eyes welled up and a single tear fell down his cheek and onto his blazer.

"I was devastated. And I was angry. I was angry that I missed it. I missed her entire life. I was angry at Magdalen for not trying harder to find me—to tell me about her.

"Eventually, I understood that it was I who deserved the blame. I was angry with myself for not seizing that one moment, for not following Elsa back to her mother and presenting myself right then and there. Casting myself at her feet and asking her to take me, poor professor that I was at the time."

He swallowed, letting the emotion wash over him as he remembered.

Elizabeth stared at her hands and waited for him to continue.

"When we met later in life, I chose not to pain her with the memory, to force a conversation that she clearly was not ready to have with me. I could not be selfish with her. And it would have been selfish."

He took a deep breath, "She was the love of my life. My beloved."

As he spoke, Elizabeth could see it all play like a movie. Like she was inside his head reliving the memory with him.

She reached out and clasped his hand bringing it down to the space on the wooden bench between them. They both studied *Le Penseur* once more with shining eyes.

After a few minutes of replaying what he'd said, something struck her, "Matthieu did you say propose to her *again?*"

He smiled, letting it touch his still gleaming eyes. "Yes. I proposed to her many times. In fact, this," he signaled to the space they inhabited, "is where I proposed to her for the first time." His eyes twinkled.

Then he laughed, "And the first time she refused."

His was a throaty, infectious kind of laugh. She found herself sharing in his enjoyment, his memory of their tenacious, strong-willed Mags.

Elizabeth didn't have time to think about why Mags had refused or what it meant that Matthieu had continued to ask; she didn't have time to dwell on their sad love story because Matthieu soon took her hand and brought her to her feet with surprising strength.

"Walk with me, Lizzie," he placed her hand into the crux of his elbow and walked back out towards the roses. "I know that you thought you had a message to deliver to me, but as it happens I have a message for you."

Elizabeth's head was swimming with all that she'd just learned. *Matthieu knew about Elsa. He'd spoken to her.* He'd loved Mags so much that he'd refused to push her. Beth wondered what her great-aunt would say if she'd known; how she would feel that they'd actually met before their daughter died. How Matthieu had recognized himself in Elsa's face.

Matthieu slowed in front of a vibrant bush of pink roses and turned her to face him.

"You see, Lizzie," he said gently, hesitating.

He took both of her hands in his before continuing. "Brian did find your father."

Elizabeth shook her head clear, trying to adjust to the new direction in the conversation; she'd expected to hear more about her great-aunt, but he was suddenly talking about her father? She let the question show in her eyes.

Matthieu nodded, seeing her confusion and launched into the story. "Your mother Carolina came to France for a time in her twenties and had a love affair with a young man of similar age." His lovely accent vacillated between British and French in a melodious way.

She shook her head again, forcing herself to actually focus on what he was saying, where he was going; she'd already known this about her mother.

He continued, "They thought they had successfully kept it a secret, but we always suspected. Brian approached me several weeks ago and we devised a plan to deduce the validity of those long held suspicions.

"Brian compared your DNA with the DNA of the man's sister, your aunt, who was fully aware of what Brian was trying to do."

He took a deep breath, a sense of excitement transformed his beautifully wrinkled face, "Her brother is your father."

Elizabeth's heart pounded violently in her ears. Everything in front of her seemed to freeze in place. She stopped breathing.

Until finally Matthieu broke into a brilliant smile, "His name is Alexandre . . . Alexandre *Fleury*, my nephew."

CHAPTER 5: FAMILY

Elizabeth stared at Matthieu, barely blinking.

She could see his puffed up eyebrows and silver hair, but the words that had just come from his mouth, made him seem very far away. Like he was on the other side of a thick glass wall.

The plan that Mags had for her, the road she had sent her down—at times it seemed so intricate, that it was difficult to see the way. Elizabeth had stopped trying to figure it out long ago.

But now, standing there at Musée Rodin in Paris, facing a man she had been sent to find, who now also turned out to be . . . her own flesh and blood? Things were starting to become crystal clear.

Family.

It was just as Mags had designed.

How well she had known Elizabeth. Known how to guide her. What to say and when to say it, to drive her there. To that moment.

Now that she looked into his face, she could see that his hazel eyes were actually a faded shade of green. A shade or two lighter than her own.

Slowly, a smile started to rise. It transformed first her lips, then her cheeks, and then finally, it touched her eyes. In that moment it all came together.

It was as if she had been driving down a dark road, the car lights illuminating only one hundred feet at a time.

She had accepted that she had placed herself on a dark road when she had chosen the law all those years ago. The letters that Mags had left behind had simply turned on the headlights.

But now, the sun had risen and she could see *everything*. She could see exactly where Mags had always planned to take her. Her final destination.

To reveal all, to show her the good in the world, to reunite her with her family.

Elizabeth found her voice, "Then that means . . . Matthieu you're . . . my great-uncle?" She looked away from him, towards the flowers. "Just like Mags was my great-aunt?" Her eyes found a large, perfectly shaped red rose as she continued to think through the ramifications of what he had just said.

She continued, "So you were never married, but you are my great-uncle anyway?" She looked back at him and started to laugh.

In photography, and any art, really, she'd always loved symmetry. It went beyond basic composition principles,

Elizabeth *loved* it. The way trees could frame a lake . . . the way Broadway intersected Times Square in New York . . . a butterfly. . . .

She thought it was the most beautiful expression in nature and the mark of a truly great plan.

The symmetry of the moment took her breath away. She continued to giggle as Matthieu held her hands, his own beautiful smile and bright eyes, understanding.

She dropped his hands and threw her arms around him. They both shook with the force of their laughter and delight as they embraced each other as family for the first time.

She withdrew so that she could see his face again. "So then Alexandre doesn't know about me? He's never known about me? Where does he live? What does he do? Do I have any siblings? Is he married? Where is he now? When are you planning on telling him? Do you think he'll want to meet me?"

All the questions she'd kept bottled up for fear that Brian wouldn't have the answers now manifested as an avalanche headed straight for Matthieu. Even so, they were more to satisfy her intellectual curiosity. Finding out that Matthieu was her great-uncle was enough in the way of family.

"My Dear, my Dear." He took her hands again. "We have time now. I'm not going to disappear and leave you without your answers." He let their arms sway between them.

"I am quite excited to welcome you into our family and so is your aunt, my niece, Emily. It was she who provided the DNA sample."

"I have an aunt?" she repeated, remembering what he had said before, but relishing in the news again.

"Your father is an artist—he's quite well known in Paris," Matthieu continued. "As a matter of fact, he has a show this Friday. He's an eccentric, a bit of a curmudgeon actually. Emily and I thought it best to wait until *after* Friday. He's a good man, to be sure, but he can be a bit barmy before a show. Best not to add a variable into the mix now." He wiggled his eyebrows mischievously.

She was definitely a variable.

"He lives in Méré a little village less than an hour from central Paris, but he also has an apartment and studio here. We have a family Château in Méré. It's where I live as well. *Château Fleury.*"

Just then their little private reunion bubble burst as a steady flow of tourists walked through the gate behind them. Elizabeth took in their walking shoes and backpacks, tourists ready for a day of sightseeing and schoolchildren on a visit to the museum.

"Matthieu," she began, "I don't know what you have planned, but I would really like to spend more time speaking to you, would that be all right?" she asked tentatively.

"Of course. I have no plans today, Lizzie." He smiled at her.

"Well in that case, would you and Brian consider coming back to the place where I'm staying, my boyfriend's apartment?" The word sounded wrong somehow, "Boyfriend? That sounds odd at thirty-five," she mused out loud.

Matthieu laughed, "Try explaining a girlfriend you only speak to in letters when you're eighty!" His eyes twinkled.

"So then you never married?" she asked.

"No. Magdalen was the love of my life. She used to call me an idealist . . . a romantic. I suppose it's true. I'd found company throughout my days here and there, but no one could compare to her."

He stared at the red roses, clearly lost in some private memory of the woman they both loved. Little French children walked by speaking animatedly about the flowers, breaking them both out of their reverie.

"Let's continue this conversation at your apartment, shall we? I'll reconnect with Brian and update him on our progress." And with that Matthieu walked back towards the entrance.

She was so excited, her skin felt like it was actually vibrating. Reaching into her black shoulder bag, she extracted her phone, dialing Connor with shaking fingers.

He answered on the first ring, "Lara." It was a loving caress on his lips.

"Connor!" She half yelled into the phone.

"What's wrong?" His voice thickened with concern instantly. He was so quick to jump to alarm these days, she was surprised by the direction of his thoughts.

"No, no nothing." She assured him. "I'm just excited."

"Oh," he relaxed into the phone. "Good, that's good." His voice was still strained, but she could hear him exhale on the other end.

"It turns out that Matthieu isn't just a pseudo great-uncle—he really *is* my great-uncle! His nephew Alexandre Fleury is my father, isn't that amazing?!"

She didn't wait for him to respond. She launched herself head first into the story, giving him a play-by-play. Describing what she had thought, what she had felt walking up to him.

How they hadn't even introduced each other initially, just started talking like old friends. She took him through the entire experience minute by minute until he was all caught up.

She hadn't realized it, but she had started to pace in front of the roses. Several people were giving her sidelong glances as they stared at a map of the gardens, orienting themselves.

Lowering her voice she continued, "Anyway, I want to take Matthieu and Brian back to the apartment and maybe use the theatre to show the video that Mags left for Matthieu. Would that be OK?"

"What are you asking?" He sounded confused.

Hadn't she just said?

"To take them back to the apartment?" she repeated.

"Lara, it's your apartment as well. Why are you asking for permission?"

"Well because—" she was about to launch into the obvious fact that it was his space, but she didn't want to ruin the moment by going down that road again. Instead, she opted for a different route. "Because it's . . . *courteous*," she landed on the right word.

"We share the space and I'm just letting you know. It's just good manners, isn't it?" Her phrasing made her sound a little Irish.

He laughed into the phone, knowing full well where her thoughts had taken her, recognizing the save she'd concocted.

She smiled, secretly loving how well he knew her.

"Well all right then." He was amused. "Fancy some company? Or would a fourth person throw a wrench in your plan?"

"No! Of course you should come, I'd love for you to meet them. I'd love for you to meet . . . " she took a deep breath before finishing, "*my family.*"

She had stunned herself into silence. And then repeated it, "Connor . . . I have a family!" Her glee was uncontrollable.

A little French girl of maybe eight with a blonde ponytail scrunched her eyebrows together and pursed her lips, staring at Beth as she walked by. Her little hands clutched the strap of her sack.

"Yes, you do," he said into the phone. But there was something else behind his words. A hint of sadness? She was probably reading into things.

"I'll see you all back there in about an hour," he finished.

"Perfect!" she smiled. "Oh, and Connor?"

"Yes, Lara?"

"I love you."

She heard him smile over the phone.

"Matthieu are you sure you wouldn't rather see this on your own first? Brian and I can go to the kitchen and wait for you there. You just need to double-click on this video and then you can open the other folders after that. Whatever you want to do. Mags left this for you." Beth checked in with her great-uncle one final time.

"Nonsense! We are all family here." He smiled and leaned back in one of the dark leather theatre seats facing the screen.

He placed his elbows on the armrests and clasped his hands in front of his mouth, waiting.

Brian sat next to him smiling and nodding in encouragement. He had been delighted that Matthieu and Elizabeth had gotten on so well. And was more than happy to join them back at Connor's apartment, clearly enjoying how the master plan he and Mags had created together was playing out.

Like a story they had planned; carefully crafted, setting things in motion, and now the people and places were coming together in ways they could not have fully foreseen.

"OK," she was satisfied that they weren't intruding on Matthieu's special message from Mags.

She had connected her laptop to the entertainment center that projected images onto the screen. She took a deep breath before double clicking the file that read *Matthieu My Love START HERE*. The file took a second to load giving Elizabeth an opportunity to take the seat on Matthieu's right.

A picture formed of the bright blue couch in the living room of the house she had grown up in with Mags in Berkeley.

Mags fiddled with her computer and sat on the couch. She wore a flowing white Bohemian top. Her silver hair was perfectly combed with loose curls. She had made an effort with her makeup as well.

Beth smiled, she'd never seen this side of Mags. Getting dolled up for the man she loved.

She sat on the couch and fiddled with her hair the way people tend to do when they don't realize they are already being filmed.

Elizabeth especially enjoyed seeing Mags like this, *human*, self-conscious and sometimes flawed.

"Oh, I think it's already started, OK." She crossed her ankles bringing her legs tightly together and folding her hands in her lap.

She smiled.

Something in Beth's chest stirred, how she had missed that smile.

"Matthieu, my Darling," she started.

"I'm so very glad to know that you and my Lizzie have finally met. I hope that after your conversation," she hesitated, *"after what she told you about the secret I had been keeping from you, that—that you don't hate me."*

Her voice broke.

"I thought about finding you when Elsa was little, to tell you about her, to share her with you, all the time. But it wasn't easy as a single mother running my own business in Spain, and I didn't want you to change your life, as I knew you would.

"I trusted that things would work out the way they were supposed to. And then I lost Elsa . . . " her voice broke on Elsa's name.

Her lips drew together, her eyes watered. She brought her right hand to her mouth and swallowed, trying not to break down.

"It took . . . it took a very long time for me to heal enough to experience the good in life again. And when we found each other that first time, I was just so relieved to have you back in my life. It's what I needed, you were what I needed.

"I wasn't ready to tell you, to share her with you because then I would have to face what I had lost. Again.

"And then the next time, well, life had moved on and so that second time I didn't tell you because I didn't want to cause you pain. Maybe I was still being selfish then, but it was a choice I made.

"I'm sorry."

She looked at her hands.

"And then the last time," she gave the camera a sad smile, "in Paris I thought that, we might never see each other again, and selfishly I didn't want our ending to be a bad one. To risk your never speaking to me again."

She stopped, reaching to the side table with the lamp to grab a tissue.

She dabbed her eyes before continuing, "I'm sorry for all of it. While my reasons for not telling you changed over the last several decades, at the heart of it, I was wrong."

She laughed a little through the tears, "If my Lizzie ever sees this, she might fall out of her chair. But it's true, I was wrong—I should have told you.

"We should have looked at pictures together. We should have cried together. We should have held each other and marched forward together. I'm sorry."

She used the Kleenex, laughing again. "The funny thing, or maybe the irony is a better way to put it, is that I had finally plucked up the courage—the determination to come to Méré and tell you in person.

"Some years ago I bought a Château in Millemont, I was going to surprise you. I thought that maybe in the end we could have a bit of happiness together. Maybe share a life in the way that we both always dreamed. So I was planning on installing myself in Millemont and then showing up at your door. It was a plan I set in motion years ago, but never executed. It was somehow enough that I had it there, in my back pocket waiting for me."

She let out a sad little laugh. "But then, the day I was finally going to book the one-way ticket—I got the call. Turns out I had another one-way ticket with my name on it."

She smiled into the camera as the tears welled-up. "Isn't that just a kick in the ass?" she laughed, honestly. The tears streamed down her face.

Elizabeth wiped her own tears with the back of her hand, laughing a little with Mags.

"Anyway, I hope that this memory card set some things right. Although it was some time ago, I suspected that you knew about Elsa, about what happened to her. If that's true and you knew all along . . . " she trailed off shaking her head, her eyes focused on her hands.

She looked back into the camera, "I'm sorry."

She gave the camera a little shrug.

"I hope that you and my Lizzie are together now. And that my suspicions about Alex were correct. And if not . . . who am I kidding . . . of course he's her father! There's no other possibility. Which means that you, my love, are also my Lizzie's uncle.

"Tell her that I love her and give her a big hug for me."

Mags wiped the tears from her cheeks with her fingertips quickly before continuing, "This memory card has all the pictures I could find of Elsa and even the few home videos that I shot from back then.

"It's my last attempt to share her with you. Cowardly, I know," she shook her head, *"giving all of this to you now that I'm dead, but there it is."*

Then she grew quiet, looking off past the camera towards the window.

Beth knew what she would see, the little park with beautiful mature trees and a small garden, directly across the street from their little house in Berkeley.

"But you know everything happens for a reason. Now. Here. At the end I think it all happened the way it was supposed to, you know? Maybe this will all help my Lizzie find her way. I hope you and Alexandre and Emily enjoy her. She is marvelous," she smiled at the camera, most of her tears now wiped away.

"All right!" She waved her hands like she'd had enough of her own blubbering.

She looked straight into the camera, "I'm sorry Matt, truly I am. I hope that when you are at your end you will look back on our time—our great love story and think fondly of me. I love you."

A single tear fell down her cheek.

She gulped.

"Elsa and I will be waiting."

Nodding, she brought her right hand up to her lips and blew him a kiss.

Next to Beth, Matthieu extended his arm into the air and caught it.

After the emotional video, Elizabeth had gotten up to pass the tissues.

They all looked at each other and laughed at the state of their faces. Mags certainly knew how to bring the house down.

Elizabeth looked up past Brian and Matthieu who were still sitting in the theatre seats, towards the shelves in the back.

Connor was leaning against the wall near one of the bookcases. His face was wet with tears also.

Elizabeth smiled at him, glad he had been able to see it with her. To experience it with them.

He brought his shoulder up to his cheek, using his black dress shirt to dry his face.

He started moving towards her. She walked around the theatre seats and met him halfway.

Connor drew her into his arms and she was glad for it. She relaxed into the warmth of his embrace, burying her face in his chest.

After a long moment she let him go, taking his hand instead and pulling him towards Brian and Matthieu. She made all the introductions.

Connor's voice was thick with emotion, "Nothin' like a good woman to bring a man to his knees!" He shook his head, still using his dress shirt to wipe the moisture from his face.

Matthieu and Brian laughed heartily at that, nodding in agreement.

"I think we could all use some wine. . . ." Elizabeth said as the last wave of emotion settled.

"Or some whiskey," Connor added.

They went through the rest of the SD card, including Elsa's home videos. They watched her walking around a little apartment in Madrid as a toddler, waddling around here and there in a tiny white dress. Also riding a bike, playing soccer in the park, singing a song in Spanish, blowing out the candles on her fifth birthday cake—which was several layers tall and had blue and green frosting.

Elizabeth put the pictures folder on slide show mode. They all laughed together here and there with the pictures of the little girl that Mags and Matthieu had created so long ago.

Pictures of her sticking her tongue out, her dressed up for Halloween, her doing a handstand. Pictures of her and a young Mags together, embracing each other cheek to cheek.

Pictures of them facing each other holding hands and twirling. Pictures of Mags sitting on a park bench watching Elsa, of Elsa with other little kids and some women who were a little younger than Mags.

It took them two hours to get through it all. At some point Connor had slipped out to order a late lunch for their guests. They served themselves in the kitchen afterwards, all standing and talking animatedly.

Matthieu spoke to them about Château Fleury and Méré, about his parents, Jean and Marie Fleury and how he purchased the Château for them some forty years before.

He told them how his parents and his one sibling, his older brother Luc—Alexandre's father—had been deceased for many years. He recounted how he had split his time between teaching in London and living in Méré.

How Alexandre had done the same between Méré and Paris, and how Beth's aunt Emily also lived in a smaller house up the street. She'd moved there after her second husband had died.

Apparently, Alexandre was divorced. He'd always put his art first and never had kids. He had lived with several women over the years, the last of which he'd remained with for the better part of a decade until she had lost her battle with cancer, two years before.

Matthieu told her about her three cousins, Liliane, Renée, and Bridgett.

Elizabeth drank it all in, hearing all about the family she never knew she had. The family she hoped to know.

Matthieu told her that he and Emily had decided to tell Alexandre at dinner on Sunday night at Château Fleury.

He invited them all to dinner, but warned that Alexandre leaned towards the melodramatic. He was a true artist ruled by his emotions and there was no telling what they might get from him.

"Perhaps a loud outburst, or some light sobs . . . or he might just get up and throw himself into his work again—you never know with him. But he's got the biggest heart, Lizzie. I'm sure in the end he will be very glad to know you," he assured her.

Before walking through the door, Matthieu turned to her mischievously, "If you would like, come by the opening of his show, if you're curious, that is." He lowered his head a degree, like he was looking at her from behind a pair of spectacles, "We just won't make any introductions then." He winked.

Once they had gone, Elizabeth turned to Connor with wide eyes, her mouth open, "I have a family! I'm not alone in the world."

She shook her head, disbelieving. She brought her palms up to her cheeks, her brain trying to process all that had happened.

Connor took her hands from her face and held her gaze, "Lara, you haven't been alone since first I laid eyes on you. You were my family since the day you set foot in Ireland."

CHAPTER 6: THE APARTMENT

Elizabeth was lying on the couch in the living room the following day, her laptop on her belly.

She had just Googled her father. Apparently, he was a pretty big deal in the Parisian art world, successfully putting on shows for the better part of forty years.

He dabbled in everything from paintings to sculptures and installations, and had even tried his hand at performance art in the eighties.

Closing the laptop, she moved it from her stomach to the small glass coffee table to her right just as the door opened.

"Lara luv, are you here?"

Elizabeth shot an arm into the air and waved from the couch so he could see her.

She heard him lay his things down on the floor, before walking over to the small armchair next to the couch. He leaned back into the chair so that his neck rested on the top. He closed his eyes and for several minutes they shared the space in silence.

Elizabeth was lost in her own thoughts, imagining what her father's opening night might look like.

She thought about that first meeting when their eyes would meet. The article she had read online confirmed what Matthieu had said, he was an eccentric who leaned towards the dramatic.

But he'd spent a great deal of his free time volunteering; teaching classes to kids with special needs; painting a mural for the children's ward at a local hospital.

Google images on him ranged from stark, serious portraits, to playful candid pictures of him painting with children and laughing with puppies.

Beth turned to face the art along the wall between the windows, examining the lines of the drawing directly in front of the couch, sandwiched between a beautiful Degas dancer and a powerfully dreamy Chagall. It was a sketch of an Antonio Canova marble sculpture which she knew well, *Psyche Revived by Cupid's Kiss.*

It had always moved her, she even had a small replica of the statue sitting on the desk in her San Francisco office.

She'd often stared at it and wondered what her life could be like outside of those white walls. It always snapped her out of the gray life—so much so that she had a slightly larger version of it in her bedroom at the apartment in the Marina.

How peculiar that Connor had chosen that same image to decorate the living room. She smiled, basking in the coincidence—the symmetry of life.

She would never have imagined that she would be lying on a couch in Paris staring at the same sculpture that had been the cause of so many daydreams, living with a gorgeous Irishman and meeting a new family.

Her fingers caressed the white couch beneath her. It was very much her style as well.

Then there was the colorfully bright photograph of the rolling Tuscan hills in Italy, the sun setting over a small house in the distance. It hung in the kitchen between the cabinets and the fridge. She'd pinned that same image several weeks ago to her Pinterest board.

Something was starting to click, quickly she sat up taking in the space again with new eyes. She thought about the framed album cover in the theatre room.

It had a man standing on a vast plane, a water tower behind him, a large balloon more than twice his size in his left hand above. The title, "The Weatherman," was written in big lettering above the balloon.

It was by Gregory Alan Isakov and just happened to be one of her favorite records.

She thought about the finishes to the house—the chandeliers—they were all pieces she would have chosen for herself.

Even the glassware in the kitchen was to her taste. In fact, she'd stopped in a shop in London several weeks before and nearly purchased the exact same set of glassware that now occupied the cabinets in their Paris kitchen. She'd recognized the Celtic knot design etched in the bottom of the glass, but had thought nothing of it.

She looked over at her Irishman, "Connor? Is there a *reason* there's so much of me in this apartment? Or do we just have shockingly similar tastes?"

"Is it your taste?" he asked, too innocently, without opening his eyes. "I'm so glad you like it," he said nonchalantly.

She narrowed her eyes and stared at him until he finally looked back at her.

He shook his head and shrugged his shoulders, "I may have taken your taste into consideration. Is there something wrong with that?" He raised an eyebrow, daring her to take issue with what anyone else would consider a nice gesture from their loving boyfriend.

She waited for him to explain. Her stoic expression firmly frozen in place.

Finally, he threw up his hands, "Oh all right, you win. I more than took your tastes into consideration. I may have had an interior designer investigate what you liked."

"Investigate?"

"Yes."

She shook her head and moved her hands in an *I'm going to need more* gesture.

"Well . . . he may have looked in on your social media accounts to see what you liked. He may have hired people to look into your design choices in San Francisco." He shook his head again too innocently.

She remembered the well-dressed man in the indigo shirt, taking pictures of the London Glass shop where she'd first examined the glassware with the Celtic knot. She'd thought she was being paranoid . . . was he the interior designer?

"Did he look into my buying habits in London as well?"

Connor shook his head considering, "Maybe?" He looked guilty.

"You had someone following me?" her voice rose.

"It wasn't like that, he was only supposed to look in on you and get a sense for what you liked!" He was defensive.

"Wow." She sat bolt upright. "You kind of stalked me!"

She looked out past the art, to the window, "Geez . . . am I ever alone? Brian was keeping tabs on me, so were you, and now I find out that some strange interior designer was cyber stalking me and following me around London as I shopped?"

"Some people might classify that as stalking, others might see it as a gesture of love." He tried and failed to get her to see things his way.

She tilted her head and gave him her *oh come on* look.

"OK!" he threw up his hands again, "Maybe I stalked you a little."

He came over to the couch. Still standing he leaned down to kiss her. She let him, but didn't kiss back.

The number of people keeping tabs on her in London was unnerving and a complete departure from her liberating time traveling around Ireland. Part of her missed the Gypsy life, traipsing around completely unencumbered. It wasn't the first time she wondered whether a life by Connor's side would mean the loss of certain freedoms she'd only just reacquired for herself. But Brian had been Mags' doing. . . . And all of it had been for honorable purposes.

He sat on the couch and brought her bare legs across his lap, "Do you really mind, Luv? I was only trying to make this place feel like your home. I want you to think of it as your apartment, because it is."

His eyes were so genuine, so heartbreakingly sincere—he had only aimed to please—that she couldn't stay angry.

In truth, so much had happened that was out of her control since January that she had stopped giving any real weight to the things that just didn't matter.

Still, the situation gave rise to a question that would continue to live in the back of her mind . . . whether commitment meant a loss of freedom. She wondered if she should allow the question to flee to the corners of her mind so easily, whether she should fight harder to think through the very real possibility that being with Connor might be too much. But then she looked at his beautiful blue eyes. And her heart melted. So, much like she had that first morning when Mona had woken her with the vacuum cleaner, Elizabeth gave up being mad.

"Am I forgiven?" he asked, giving her puppy dog eyes and a frown.

"Yes," she relented, pushing away all other thoughts and holding onto his good intentions. "But only because you are ridiculously hot and I'm in love with you."

Her tease made him grin wildly. "Good, because I plan to keep on stalking you *forever*." His eyes grew wide on the last word. Then he reconsidered, "I didn't mean to sound like a nutter just then, can I have a do over?"

She nodded, "Good choice."

She narrowed her eyes, "Forever is a long time anyway." She looked back towards Psyche and Cupid.

Connor stroked her legs, "Not long enough, Lara."

She looked back into his eyes, falling into them, feeling his intensity. It felt like he was trying to tell her something. Whatever it was, it threw her, thrilled her . . . terrified her.

She shook her head, breaking eye contact. Looking for a reason to change the subject, she said the first thing that came to mind, "I can't believe I never asked you this, but how did you get your hands on this place? With those views, I can't imagine anyone giving it up."

It wasn't always a question of money in a city as old as Paris, often it was a question of availability. And a penthouse like Connor's was bound to draw several buyers.

"Well do you remember when I left you in Ireland after we went to go see Fungie?"

She nodded.

"Well I had to leave that day because they'd moved up the auction for this place. I had my eye on it for a few weeks before that. In fact, I came to Paris after we went to the Cliffs of Moher for the express purpose of having a look see." He looked up at the ceiling, taking in the details.

"So I came back for the auction after we had gotten together, and gone to see Fungie," he started again. "It was a steal and such a find." His eyes grew bright the way they always did when he talked about finding an undiscovered treasure.

"It belonged to the same woman who'd lived here since the thirties. She was the mistress of a successful business person in Paris and this was their love nest," he smiled at her.

"And then," he continued, "after the owner passed away, the estate installed a tenant here for many years. When she died the apartment was put up for auction by the French government to cover debts. It's called, Une vente à la bougie, or sale with a candle."

She shook her head glad for the interesting, but light, turn in their conversation. "Why?"

"It's called that because centuries ago, a candle was lit when the lot was put up for sale and the candle was blown out when the final bid was made. Someone would announce 'Sold!' and that would be that. They still light a candle to this day. It's quite an event to watch, let alone participate in."

"So then you bought it and renovated it, basically all in the time that we've known each other?"

He nodded, "Yes."

His eyes grew intense again. His voice grew low, conspiratorial. "You want to know a secret?"

"OK," she said tentatively, not certain she did. His voice had taken on that same intensity that made her feel like he was about to throw them both over a cliff.

He read the fear in her eyes, but continued in spite of it. Connor knew he'd have to push her bit by bit. To get her to start understanding his intentions, his wishes for their future. "I bought this place because I could see you in it. I could see a life for us here."

Elizabeth tried to ignore the implication of such a statement, biting her lip and looking away, "Didn't you just say that you first saw it right after we met?" she said with a laugh, trying to keep things light.

He nodded, but said nothing.

"And then you bought it . . ." she thought through what he was saying, "after just a few days together?"

He reached for her hand. "Yes. I knew Lara. *I've known* since you walked into my mother's cottage. Haven't I always told you that?"

His eyes were as deep and serious as ever. She could feel her chest rising and falling and the loud pounding in her ears. His wasn't a look of hunger or lust, it was a look of love and devotion.

Of commitment.

The blood rose to her face, the conversation had grown too serious. She couldn't think about what happened next.

Not yet.

She changed the subject again, "Have you always liked auctions and old things?" her voice crescendoed, teasingly.

She knew the answer already, but it was the easiest way to move his mind away from heavier topics.

It worked beautifully.

His lips turned up into a smile, knowing full well what she was doing, but getting caught up in the story of how he came to be a collector regardless. He looked out towards one of the windows and launched into a tale about getting lost in history class.

And looking up the stories behind ancient swords and reading about the Holy Grail.

And spending hours talking with Kilian about where it might be now. He talked about watching the Indiana Jones films and how he had considered becoming a professor. How he had found a way to use his love of history, for antiquities in an unconventional way without being tied to academia for a job.

Then he launched into more accounts of his time in Africa. He had already told her about his most recent trip during their week and a half long hibernation in London, but there always seemed to be more to tell.

He had showed her pictures and told her about the people he met, the guide who had taken him from Kenya, to Tanzania, to Zambia.

He talked about watching the sunrise and the sunset and how he'd thought of her, wishing that she was with him. He thought about what their life might be like with him

88

tracking down rare treasures, and her with a camera in her hands. What adventures they would have.

She liked hearing him talk like this. Sometimes it felt like she was the one doing all of the talking. She'd missed hearing about his stories and getting glimpses of that childlike Connor.

Always the little boy on a quest to find rare treasures, just like when Rhia had left the treasure map for him in the woods by the lake.

Elizabeth smiled and studied his profile as he talked. Loving the way his mouth curled up into a smile here and there, or how his chest rose and fell with a laugh as he recounted memory upon memory.

And with every story, every memory, she found herself falling a little deeper in love with him.

For a second, and only a second, she considered what a lifetime with this man might look like.

She shook her head, forcing herself back to the present. She wanted to keep him talking.

"So what's the latest on the auction house then? Did those phone calls stop? The reno is done, right? When do you guys think you'll be able to move the pieces in?"

He exhaled deeply and sunk back into the couch letting his head rest on top of the white tufts.

She'd intended to hold onto her childlike Connor, but she realized too late that the question would force him to be grown-up Connor.

"I don't know, Lara. It's one big headache after another. The paperwork here, the security issues, the shit we haven't yet seen. The other two houses were definitely easier to set up." He didn't just sound frustrated, he sounded concerned.

"You could always set it up and then sell it, be done with the hassle," she offered.

"I suppose I could. But to be fair, it really isn't setting up the house that is bothering me. It's the security issues. . . ." his voice trailed off.

Then he sat up all at once turning to face her on the couch. "Lara, I think it's Stephen."

She sat up then too, drawing her knees to her chest. "What do you mean?" The direction of his thoughts felt abrupt, like something had been weighing on him and he couldn't take it anymore.

"Why do you say that?" she asked quickly not waiting for an answer to her previous question.

"Well it started with the phone calls, right? Then there was the vandalism, and we've got all that sorted, but . . . there's just something about this harassment, and we both know he's unstable. I'm worried, especially for you."

"For me?" she was genuinely taken aback. "The harassment is coming at you, I'm worried about you Connor. This is nothing to do with me."

They both grew silent. She searched for an explanation. "Maybe it's just some idiot kids or some crazy person—some woman you blew off."

He shook his head, "No, this feels very targeted."

"Well," she considered a solution, "just up the security at Bannon's and keep documenting everything like you have been."

He looked at her considering and deciding what to say next. "I had a PI on him Lara, since the day he was released. But he's lost track of him. I think I'm going to hire some extra security for you as well."

She shook her head, "That isn't necessary. It probably doesn't have anything to do with me. It isn't him." She felt certain.

Connor gave her a measured look. "Still, I'm hiring the security. If it is Stephen, he's dangerous, he could come at you at any moment."

She hugged her bare knees to her chest more tightly, "I can take care of myself."

He gave her a look of love and adoration, tilting his head the way she sometimes did, "I know you can—"

His phone started ringing, cutting him off.

"Sorry I'm going to have to take this," he said after examining the screen. "Yeah, Auguste?"

He sat up abruptly, "What?"

Then he was on his feet, "Yes, when? OK, I'll be right there."

He walked around the couch and grabbed his laptop bag, he reached the foyer before she knew what was happening.

"Connor, what's going on?"

"There's been another break-in." He froze in place, his eyebrows drew together. "Lara please promise me you'll stay in the apartment until I get back, OK?"

She didn't move.

"OK?" He was more forceful.

She'd already gone out that day. She had plenty of food and wine and chocolate—technically, there was no need to leave. But she didn't like being forced to stay in the apartment. The question that had scurried away to the back of her mind rose to the forefront . . . *freedom.*

"I'm fine," she said vaguely.

He looked at her sharply. "That may be, but I'm not taking any chances."

He waited for her to agree. His eyes started to hood over; he braved himself for whatever he would have to do or say to get her to stay safe.

She heard the urgency in his voice even as she felt the instant restlessness that accompanied any restriction on her movements . . . especially one which she viewed as wildly unnecessary.

Connor had started to radiate anxiety. She could feel the wave hit her from across the room. He was really worried.

"Fine, I'll stay put." She fought the urge to cross her fingers.

He nodded in acknowledgment quickly before disappearing into the foyer. Elizabeth heard him turn the knob and lock the apartment behind him.

Chapter 7: L'Amour

The atmosphere at Galerie Christophe just off of Rue Jacob in Saint-Germain, was electric. It was a large space with at least four separate rooms.

Her father's art took up the entire gallery.

She stood by the large windows, a glass of champagne in one hand, the other wrapped around her own waist, fiddling with the silky fabric of her black cocktail dress.

Surreptitiously, she watched her father mingle, kissing cheeks, shaking hands, patting backs. He appeared to be in a very good mood smiling and laughing consistently.

He was a tall man in his sixties. Quite fit for his age and for an artist for that matter. He sauntered about the room happily directing his guests to that sculpture or that painting. He had an easy air about him.

Connor appeared at her elbow, "If you keep watching him like that, he's going to come over and then he might figure it out."

"What do you mean, *figure it out?* He doesn't even know I exist!" She sipped her champagne nervously.

Connor lowered his voice as Alexandre moved to speak to a group closer to where they were standing by the window. "Have you seen the man's eyes? The same exact shade of green."

He wrapped his arm around her waist, resting his hand on her hip. She covered it with her fingers, grateful for his presence.

Every once in a while Alexandre did something that reminded her of herself, tilting his head and waiting for a response or the way he moved his hands when he talked. It was surreal, seeing herself in a stranger.

The gallery was packed with elegant men and women, mostly in black, some in white, a few in bright colors.

It was a truth universally known, that black was the favored color of all Parisians.

True to form, Alexandre was dressed in a black dress shirt, black blazer, and black slacks, like most of the men in the room. But, he wore patent royal blue shoes that shined with the gallery lighting and a strikingly vivid blue tie to match.

Elizabeth locked eyes with Matthieu as he stood in one corner drinking champagne with Brian and another woman.

Beth acknowledged them with a pleasant nod and a tip of her glass.

They smiled in response. The woman looked at her curiously, with a steady smile. She had perfect brown hair that came down past her shoulders; it was curled in elegant waves. She wore a fitted black and white dress. Beth rightly supposed that the woman was in her sixties, like Alexandre.

She had kind eyes and a slender frame. Elizabeth gave her a short wave. The woman nodded and held up her champagne glass as Beth had just done.

Matthieu mouthed the word "Emily". Beth had guessed as much, this was her aunt, the one who had supplied the DNA that had confirmed that her brother, Alexandre Fleury, was her father.

The threesome continued to look at Elizabeth and Connor across the room until Alexandre himself approached them in the corner.

Quickly, they all composed themselves making sure not to look in the couple's direction again.

Elizabeth wandered around the gallery taking in the versatile pieces.

Most exhibitions of an artist's work centered on a theme, but she could not tell what the theme to this exhibition was.

There were sculptures of everyday life and paintings of crude scenes, landscapes and art installations. It was modern with throwbacks to practically everything. Picasso, Monet, Mondrian, Dali, and on and on.

There were sculptures made of modern day things: staplers, lamps, chandeliers.

It was the most eclectic mix of work she'd ever seen in one space by a single artist.

Some of it was disturbing, like a black and white photograph of a woman. She was topless with tears streaming down her face, looking directly to the camera.

Some of it was quite serene, a palette knife painting of a quiet scene in an old park with a carousel.

Apparently, the more established you were on the art scene, the less important a unifying theme was to a show.

It was odd to walk through room after room of work that had originated in her father's brain. That, at least genetically, she had some tie to it all.

After an entire lifetime of thinking that her father was a cowardly, awful uptight businessman who had left her to fend for herself, it was a revelation to be walking amongst so many beautiful pieces of art, born in the imagination of the man who had actually helped to create her.

Connor walked with her, viewing the art at her pace. When they both stopped to look at a sculpture of three lamps molded together like a snake with a crystallized rose blooming out of the top, she turned to him, "So where is he?"

His eyebrows drew together, "Who? Your father?" He did a quick search, angling his head this way and that.

She shook her head, not looking at him. "The plain clothes bodyguard you hired to tail me," she said in a dry voice, letting her annoyance seep through. She'd intended to bring it up earlier, but there hadn't been time, now she welcomed the distraction.

He exhaled roughly and ran his fingers through his hair; he knew he'd been caught and that he'd risked alienating her . . . *again*. "He's just outside. I don't know he might be sitting in a car or standing along the street keeping an eye on everyone who enters the gallery."

"It's really unnecessary," Elizabeth protested, exasperated by the whole business. "The break-in was a false alarm, nothing was taken, right?"

"No, the break-in was *not* a false alarm, it actually happened," he argued, "but yes, nothing was taken."

There was something else in his eyes. She wanted to shake it out of him, make him tell her what he wasn't saying.

"It's happening at *your* auction house, it's directed at you; it's nothing to do with me. I think it's seriously doubtful that Stephen is involved. If he wanted revenge he wouldn't come after you, he would come after me—that's what he did before. *I* was the one who embarrassed him and then *I* was the one who threw a knife into his wrist."

She stopped, taking a sip of her champagne. "No, this is something else." She shook her head, frustrated by her stubborn Irishman's obsession with her safety. He'd also started to shoulder the blame for everything. He'd certainly contributed to the original situation with Stephen when he'd given into Keanan's blood and sought revenge, but Elizabeth had been the one to take Stephen down *both* times. It was so like a man to forget that she'd been the one in control and the one Stephen had blamed.

She wasn't sure if it was the stress of the new auction house or something else entirely, but Connor seemed to carry around a near constant level of tension. She sensed a deep fear in him. It was almost as if he believed his life would be the end of hers. She could appreciate his concern for her, but his extremist nature was doing nothing to assuage her own questions regarding the relationship between commitment and freedom.

Ever since she'd discovered that he'd had her followed in London, she'd forced herself to be more aware which had caused her to spot the bodyguard immediately. Connor had neglected to mention it; he'd mentioned the *idea* of hiring extra security, but had failed to tell her he'd actually done it, let alone hired someone to follow her in plain clothes.

She would have been flat out angry, if not for the pending introduction that only happened once in a lifetime. She'd have to find a way to make him back off and calm down. Elizabeth wasn't about to start living her life irrationally afraid of her own shadow. Nothing he'd told her could lead to the conclusion that his problems at the auction house had anything to do with her.

"Well either way," he put an arm around her waist, "You're indulging me on this," he said at her ear, frustration and anger colored his voice.

He was frustrated? Clearly they were not on the same page.

She turned to him, searching his face for more information. His anger threw her—she couldn't understand it; it was irrational, none of it added up.

"You're indulging me on this," he said again more firmly. "And that's final."

He said it with such conviction, such alpha male domination that it felt like he'd punched her in the stomach.

She looked at him with such ferocity that he backtracked immediately.

He shook his head and ran his fingers through his hair again, "Jaysus, I'm sorry, Lara. I'm just—it would make me . . . I *really* can't deal with you being in danger. Please just let me have this? Let me do this my way."

She let her eyes soften because his anger had turned to a look so vulnerable that she wanted to reach up and touch his face. But the sting of his words, *that's final,* hung in the air.

Those words would never be acceptable to her; their future looked bleak indeed if he believed for a second that anything he said could exercise control over her. If, in fact, it was about control.

He could read her thoughts and tried to bridge the gap between them, visibly softening. "If it turns out to be nothing, then you can give me a big fat I told you so and we can laugh about it over treats from Jacques Genin, deal?"

She narrowed her eyes.

He tried again, "I'll even attempt to bribe the genius chocolatier to give us exclusive access or have them deliver whatever you want to the apartment for the next year."

She considered for a moment. Trying to get his words out of her head by focusing on the promise of a daily tarte au citron.

Elizabeth clinked her champagne glass against his, "Deal." She was eager to move forward and hoped the words he'd uttered were an anomaly.

They both took a sip.

Just then someone came up behind them, an antiques world acquaintance of Connor's. Elizabeth said hello to the man called Thibault and excused herself leaving the men to talk about their treasures.

After several minutes, she came across a piece in the last room of the gallery.

It was a large work that took up most of the wall, maybe six feet by six feet. It was called *L'Amour*, according to the small gray plaque which also included a price level.

She knew from overhearing a conversation that "Level Five" indicated that the piece cost at least five hundred thousand euros.

Money aside, it was the most colorful piece in the collection, composed of a series of splashes and dots in every hue of the rainbow, like a prettier Pollock.

The reds and greens and blues and yellows all mashed together in a messy, but beautiful combination of strokes and strikes. There were lines of black paint strewn throughout here and there, as well.

She thought the dark lines looked like cracks in the surface—they reminded her of pain. But the black was a very small part of the larger work, the other colors prevailed.

On the whole, it was one of the most striking pieces she'd ever seen. She stared at it for several minutes, lost in her own thoughts.

A deep male voice spoke to her right, "C'est mon préféré. Il m'a fallu presque deux ans pour terminer, mais chaque fois que je la regarde, je pense qu'il a besoin de plus."

"Perhaps it's more a sign that the subject is ever evolving," Elizabeth answered in French automatically—without taking her eyes from the piece—and without thinking about who she must be speaking to. "It's one of the most beautiful pieces I've ever seen," she finished.

She was just about to turn to the man and introduce herself when someone else came up behind him and pulled him away. He excused himself without looking back at her.

Stunned, she turned to face him as he went, realizing that she had just spoken to Alexandre Fleury.

The blood rose to her face as the encounter set in, electrifying every cell in her body.

She stood gaping until someone made an announcement and called for the guests to head back to the main space at the front of the gallery. Elizabeth and Connor filed into the room with everyone else.

A small stage had been set up along the center of the wall, between two pieces. An older man clad in an expensive gray suit introduced Alexandre, giving a mini biography of his decades of work and praising his out-of-the-box thinking, before handing the stage over to the man himself.

Alexandre clasped his hands together and welcomed everyone in French. He launched into the history of the work that he was showing. Some of the pieces had taken a decade to create others an hour. He thanked everyone again for coming to his first show in three years.

Elizabeth stopped hearing the words coming out of his mouth and started to study the man himself. Now free to look at him openly with everyone else she found herself examining all of the lines in his face, the green of his eyes, his straight eyebrows and his straight nose.

She studied his lips, they were the same as hers. Even the way he transferred his weight from one foot to the other felt familiar.

It was a strange thing indeed, to see herself so clearly in someone else. Especially someone she had always hated. But the narrative she'd been told, the narrative she had clung to was laughingly mundane next to the truth.

Her mother had come to live with Mags in France in her twenties, had an affair with a French artist, gotten back together with a previous flame upon returning to the States, lied to that man, married that man and when the truth came out he'd left her.

Instead, she was the daughter of a famous Parisian artist. How fitting to discover Alexandre after the year she'd had. She tried to imagine what a father daughter relationship might look like, but she couldn't.

She was excited to meet him, to know him, to continue to see all the strange ways in which they were similar, but she couldn't picture what it would be like to have a relationship with him.

She hoped he would want to know her, but even if he didn't it was a relief to finally know where she came from.

In truth, she had been more excited to learn that Matthieu was her great-uncle, because she loved the symmetry of Mags being her great-aunt and the love of her life, Matthieu, being her great-uncle—both by blood, not marriage.

Her *family*.

And Matthieu seemed to like her, seemed to want to know her. She continued to think in this way, not recognizing that she was already starting to build a wall between her and her newfound biological father . . . just in case.

She was so engrossed in her own thoughts that she hadn't noticed Alexandre's face change on stage.

He was a good speaker, he had done an excellent job of making eye contact with the people in the crowd, but at some point during his speech he'd laid eyes on her face— stopping there a second longer than he had meant to.

There was something oddly striking and familiar about her features.

He continued with his speech, telling a funny story about being electrocuted by one of his light sculptures, making everyone laugh.

And then he moved on to a story about a woman— the topless woman crying in the photograph in the next room. He explained that he had been walking in a small little park in Paris, when a woman had recognized and approached him.

She explained that her husband had just left her and that she was a single mother with no job. Alexandre thought she was going to ask him for money, or a job, but instead she asked him to photograph her.

She told him, "I feel naked and alone and I want you to take a picture of me. If you take a picture, then maybe my pain and desperation will disappear into the photograph. Maybe the camera will extract it from me like a poison, will you do it?"

It had taken only a minute to set up the camera and the white backdrop behind her. Without any direction from him, she took off her top and began to cry. He took one single frame.

She dressed just as quickly and with a hug goodbye and a thank you, she left his studio. Sometime later he received a letter in the mail. The woman thanked him again for the picture, and for listening to a complete stranger on that day. She'd gone home to her two daughters feeling liberated. The next day she had been offered a position at her friend's shop.

She wanted him to know that it had made a difference.

The artist then went on to talk about how art had the power to transform lives; it could bring them together, express love, process a memory, there was no limit.

How it could live in so many different forms and how it could move people to feel differently about themselves, to be different people, to strive to be better, more interesting human beings. He spoke passionately, affecting everyone in the room.

Alexandre came back to Beth's face again and again, his speech slowed every time he approached her eyes. Slowly his composed demeanor began to change until he came to the end of his speech, his voice shaking.

Halfway through his closing line he stopped, turning his entire body to face Elizabeth. The silence in the room was deafening, a couple of people started to whisper.

The man in the gray suit came up on Alexandre's side, putting a hand on his shoulder and turning to the crowd; he thanked everyone for coming, and informing them that interested buyers should find him or his staff who were wearing the gallery logo and an ear piece.

Everyone began to clap and Alexandre quickly walked out of the room.

Elizabeth was shaken. The intensity and turn in his demeanor had been so abrupt, so harsh, that she didn't know what he was seeing in her face.

Connor tightened his arm around her waist and whispered into her ear, "It'll be all right."

Elizabeth found Matthieu's group in the corner. He looked at her and shrugged. He and Emily walked out of the room after Alexandre.

Beth followed slowly behind. She had to know what was happening.

She and Connor positioned themselves near the opening of the main room, with a clear, but discrete, view of Alexandre speaking to Emily and Matthieu. Alexandre was gesticulating wildly. Elizabeth couldn't tell if he was angry or crazy.

She thought the word "Carolina" came out of Matthieu's mouth. At that Alexandre dropped his arms to his side, a look of complete surprise and understanding dawned.

"J'ai une fille?" He put his hands on his head.

Briefly, Elizabeth wondered if she ought to leave. Matthieu had been right about Alexandre being a complete wild card. She didn't know if he was going to leave his own show because of her or start yelling . . . or just stalk off.

Then he said it again, "J'ai une fille?" Matthieu nodded and Emily smiled; they both tried to look happy and reassuring.

Alexandre repeated it again "J'ai une fille? J'ai une fille? Et comment s'appelle?"

Then Beth definitely heard her name.

Her father repeated her name over and over testing the word in his mouth, and then he smiled. At that Matthieu looked over to Beth and Connor, finally. He looked relieved.

Alexandre followed Matthieu's gaze. He wore a stunned look, but his feet took him automatically towards her, in a slow but measured pace.

For a moment, Elizabeth wondered whether she looked like that when her body compelled her forward.

She could hear her heart thump loudly in her ears, the way it always did when faced with big life moments. This was it, she was about to meet her father—her real father. *For the first time.*

He stopped a couple of feet in front of her, reaching his hands out like he was about to touch her cheeks, but then he dropped his arms to his side abruptly.

"Elizabeth?" he said gently, like he was speaking to a five-year-old child.

She didn't mind, at that moment she felt like a five-year-old child.

"Yes," she answered.

For a minute, they just stared at each other. Both openly examining each other's features.

"You look very much like your mother," he said in a heavy French accent; he probably hadn't spent much time outside of France, unlike Matthieu.

He continued in a stunned tone that sounded nothing like the man he'd been on the stage moments before. "She was quite beautiful. You are quite beautiful."

"Thank you," she said automatically. Secretly pleased to meet the aesthetic approval of an artist . . . of her father.

"May I . . . *embrace* you?" he hesitated.

She wasn't sure what he was asking.

"Hug," he motioned with his hands. It sounded like *ugg*.

She reached up and hugged him without another word. Slowly he brought his arms around her.

They held each other, father and daughter occupying different mental spaces; Alexandre in an awestruck wonder and Elizabeth in a childlike place of safety.

She found herself tightening her arms around him as something—some line, some crack, some small fissure in her heart, that she didn't even know was there, healed.

She didn't know what the future held or if they would even have a relationship, but in that moment, something inside of her felt whole. She knew now where she came from, she knew now that someone had created her and *not* chosen to abandon her.

She'd gotten a bit of that back when she found out the truth about Carolina, but this one hug, this one tangible reassurance of a parental connection, was the final piece of the puzzle.

It didn't matter what happened next.

At some point they had both started to laugh, shaking with the force of it.

Many people stopped to watch the encounter, in tune to the consequence, the humanity of the moment—even if they didn't know why.

When they finally broke apart Alexandre started speaking to her in a rush of French. She nodded and smiled, agreeing to accompany him and a small party of people to dinner after the show.

Matthieu and Emily had walked over to join them and so had Brian. The six of them stood in a circle smiling and chatting happily as the art patrons walked around them, now more struck by the reunion than the art.

CHAPTER 8: PSYCHE

Elizabeth looked up at the smooth white ceiling. She was lying on what was quickly becoming her favorite couch in the living room opposite the massive windows that looked out onto Rue Vaugirard.

She'd been in a strange dreamlike state since Alexandre had hugged her in the gallery.

The rest of the show passed in a blur. Connor remained faithfully by her side, playing the dutiful boyfriend and making sure she was all right.

She went through all the polite motions of meeting people and making small talk, but when she looked back, she couldn't actually remember any of the details.

At dinner, Alexandre peppered her with questions one after the other in an excited French blur of words, completely ignoring his other guests. When she'd tried to ask him questions he rebuffed her saying that she already had a head start on knowing about his life, so it was only fair that he would be the one to ask the questions.

She told him about growing up in Berkeley, about her mother being attacked and her father leaving. She'd been delicate about why Carolina had left—it didn't seem right to have that conversation in a crowded restaurant over champagne.

Perhaps he never needed to know that piece of it. Maybe that was just for her, Carolina, Mags and now Connor.

She told him about how she'd always had a camera in her hands, but then she'd turned to the law. She told him about Yale and law school and about her lost decade.

She drilled the last ten years down to a bite-sized palatable paragraph—with a nice bright bow of positivity to wrap it all up.

Alexandre nodded smiling at everything she said, his eyes in a constant state of childlike wonder. There was a Willy Wonka quality to his features when he was excited. It was deeply gratifying for Elizabeth to experience his genuine interest in her.

She told him about Mags' passing. About going to Ireland, and then London in an attempt to find Matthieu because of the letters. At that Matthieu had looked down and smiled at his hands. He, Emily, and Brian were all listening to Elizabeth talk about her life, being new to parts of the story themselves.

Elizabeth watched all of their faces, full of love and admiration, and instant acceptance.

It was one thing to know that she had a blood bond with these people, it was another to find out that they could actually like her.

When Alexandre seemed satisfied with Elizabeth's life story, he turned to Connor. Connor dutifully answered his questions with all the flair of the Irish, making the table laugh at every turn.

They were all in good spirits. The wine and food and conversation had worked to create an infectious joy that seemed to radiate from each of their bodies.

It was a transcendent dinner. A once-in-a-lifetime experience where people from different walks of life come together for a single purpose that feels divine . . . that feels *destined.*

Her cell vibrated against the glass of the coffee table next to her, forcing her to vacate the beautiful memory of the night before. She brought the phone to her face without getting up.

A text from Connor.

Be ready at nine, Luv. And remember, dress to the nines. — *Connor*

He had planned some extravagant evening she knew nothing about. He seemed excited, though, and she was eager to spend time with him.

Eager to show up for him, since he had been so amazing throughout all of the family discoveries. Always by her side to ensure that she was comfortable.

She hoped that whatever it was, it would be fun. They needed something light to fill their Saturday night.

Absently, she scrolled through the contacts on her phone, until she found Audre and dialed the number. It rang five times before her voicemail answered.

Elizabeth left a message checking in, saying hi and informing her that they had a lot to catch up on.

Keeping in contact with her friends had become as important as developing her photography; as important as saying goodbye to the law; as important as finding Matthieu.

Audre called her back almost as soon as she finished leaving the message.

"Babes! Listen, I don't have time to talk, I know a lot happened this week, you'll just have to fill me in this next Saturday when I'm in town on business. We can do lunch and then something fun in the afternoon. Are you free?"

Before Beth could answer Audre continued, "Never mind, what am I saying? Of course you're going to make yourself free for me. I'm sure you're not going to force me to remind you of all those years you spent being a prat!"

Elizabeth laughed. Audre had made it a running joke, a running guilt trip to remind Beth just how important friendships ought to be in her new life.

Beth was glad for the reminder. It would be easy to fall into Connor and her new relatives and Paris and photography—and forget to maintain *all* of her relationships.

"Anyway Babes, I'll see you next Saturday, but quick I've got two minutes tell me you are doing something fun tonight. I'll be stuck at home drinking a glass of wine going through paperwork for the next digital installation. I need a vicarious thrill." Her voice rose, pleading.

"I don't know what I'm doing tonight. Connor said it was a surprise. All I know is I'm to dress up like I'm going to opening night at the Palais Garnier."

"Ohhhhh . . . " Audre teased her.

Elizabeth smiled, "So you know . . . we'll see. I'll fill you in. We haven't really been able to spend much time together—he's been crazy busy with Bannon's, so it'll just be good to spend some time together."

"God! I want a gorgeous Irishman to take me out for a night in Paris! OK—" she cut herself off, rushing through the rest, "Love it, love it. Have fun on your date," her voice crescendoed.

Then it turned into a strange sort of airy teasing, "I'm sure it will be . . . *magical.*"

Beth raised an eyebrow, ready to ask *what the hell was that?* But Audre filled the space again.

"OK, later Babes. Think of something fun we can do next weekend." Audre rushed off, not even bothering to say an official goodbye.

Beth stared at the screen as Audre's contact information came into view again, feeling like she'd just been thrown off of a merry-go-round that was still spinning. Classic Audre.

Elizabeth sat up and retrieved her laptop from the kitchen countertop.

It had been days since she had looked through her photographs. Now she flexed her fingers in front of her, excited to get started—excited to see what she had captured.

She needed something to occupy her brain, pass the hours until it was time to get ready for their date. And she was too much in her head to go out and look through a lens.

Usually, taking pictures was a way to escape her conscious brain and focus on the world in front of her. But today she had a feeling it would be more difficult to lose herself in the Parisian scenes—especially knowing that a bodyguard would be two steps behind her everywhere she went.

So she settled in with a box of macarons from Pierre Hermé and got to work.

Standing in front of the full length mirror inside the walk-in closet of the master, Elizabeth smoothed the bright blue fabric of her Dior gown.

It was an elegant A-line and flowed down to her ankles—a similar silhouette to the Reem Acra dress she had worn in London, but the neckline was more demure; for as sex-positive as the French were compared to Americans, they also dressed more conservatively.

Her long brown hair was curled in elegant waves, pinned on each side above her ears with two glittering combs that allowed her diamond earrings to catch the light.

She examined her bright green eyes and red lips. Just as she had done in London she drew closer to the mirror, looking deep into her own face.

She had come a very long way. She'd gone from being so full of anger and malice, determined to win at all costs—to feeling free.

For the first time in her life, she felt like she could really breathe. Everything seemed to be in its place.

She didn't know what would happen next with her family, didn't know if she would get along with her cousins or if they would think her a strange foreigner.

She didn't know where she and Connor would be in a year's time or if she would take her photography to the professional level. She didn't know if they would stay in Paris or go back to Ireland.

Nothing was certain.

Connor was her priority tonight and then tomorrow she would meet the rest of her family in the quaint little French village of Méré. Next weekend she would have lunch with Audre and that was it.

Those were the only things she knew for certain. Everything else was up in the air.

A year ago that would have driven her crazy, worse—she wouldn't have allowed for such an unbearably ambiguous future.

Now she relished in all that was to come, all that she could not foresee, all that was *possible*.

Finally, she understood the quote she had kept on the wall next to her bed in San Francisco.

She kept it there because she didn't understand it and it bothered her—not understanding. It was a quote by Albert Einstein: "The most beautiful thing we can experience is the mysterious."

Those words filled her brain as she walked out into the master, grabbing the silver clutch she had placed on the bed. She heard the front door and a moment later Connor was standing just outside the room.

He let out a low whistle, "You're stunning." He gaped at her from the doorway before striding over and kissing her cheek.

She grabbed both of his hands and gave him a once over. "You look . . . *dashing.*"

She took in his sleek black suit and dress shirt. There was a beautiful sheen to it, clearly something he had put on for the occasion.

He had left the apartment wearing something completely different. "When did you change?"

"I stopped in at a little shop, they had it ready for me." He shrugged like it was something he did regularly.

He took her hand and placed it in the crook of his elbow.

Once in the car Elizabeth began her barrage of questions. Although she had enjoyed spending the afternoon losing herself in her photography, a sense of excitement had started to bubble up inside of her.

Her curiosity had started to make focusing on anything else, difficult. She wanted to know where they were going.

"OK, we're in the car now, you can tell me, right? It's too late for the Opera, that would have started at seven-thirty . . . so *no* to the Palais Garnier," she started to reason out loud, narrowing her eyes at him.

"Hmmm . . . nine at night—the Moulin Rouge has a show that late, it includes dinner; are we going to the Moulin Rouge?" Her voice crescendoed excitedly.

He laughed and shook his head. "No gorgeous, we're going somewhere far more exclusive than the Moulin Rouge tonight."

She could see the excitement in his blue eyes and . . . *something else*. She pursed her lips and frowned hoping it would rouse him to reveal his secrets.

"You'll just have to wait and see. It's only a few more minutes." He shook his head and leaned in to kiss her neck.

She thought he would only give her a peck, but then his mouth refused to leave the spot beneath her earlobe. She turned into him, responding to his touch.

"Hey there, do you actually have a surprise for me? Or did you want us to get dressed up to make out in the car and then drive right back to the apartment?"

"I suppose we could just bypass my surprise and head back," he whispered at her throat.

She shoved him away, "Tell me!"

There was only so much mystery a girl could handle.

He took her hand and kissed her palm, he knew the gesture would relax her. "It's a surprise, Luv. Now will you please wait? For me?"

She took a deep breath and leaned back into the plush leather seat, looking out the window as the golden lights of Paris reflected on the river Seine.

He took her hand and held it on the leather seat between them. A few minutes later, the driver stopped the car in front of a huge glass pyramid, lit from within.

The Louvre.

Connor quickly got out of the car and opened her door, offering his hand as she stared past him at the glass.

"No!" She looked at the Louvre and then back at Connor. "No, Connor you didn't! Did you—did you pull a Harry Potter? Did you bribe a guy so we could make out in front of the *Mona Lisa*?"

"No," he laughed, shaking his head. "Not even I could just *bribe* a guy into getting exclusive night access to this place."

She waited, too stunned to cross-examine him.

He rolled his eyes and sighed, like it was such a chore to divulge his secrets, but she knew he was loving her reaction. "Audre knows *several* people and after giving a hefty donation they allowed it. It's all above board."

He took her hand and led her towards the main entrance where a security guard with an ear piece was waiting. He escorted them inside the glass pyramid and ushered them into the open-air cylindrical elevator. He pushed a button at waist level, like he was piloting something out of Star Trek, and down they went.

As the streets of Paris disappeared from view, Connor leaned down and whispered, "Although . . . we could make out in front of the *Mona Lisa*, if you like."

He thought he had said it quietly enough, but in the silent expanse of the elevator, the security guard snickered.

The elevator came to a stop at the bottom, the guard opened the small exit doors, and they stepped out into the Louvre.

They moved through the main lobby entrance where most of the tourists would normally gather to check their bags or make a plan, and into the next hall.

He pulled her towards the first floor of the Denon Wing, towards the Grande Galerie that housed the Italian Masters.

When they entered the galerie, she was surprised to find a small table with two champagne glasses framed by an array of treats ranging from macarons to chocolate éclairs to colorful fruit tartes.

In addition to all of the great works that could normally be found in the Grande Galerie, there was also a man in a tuxedo standing quietly in the corner, a violin in his hand. Connor nodded and the tuxedoed man began to play.

The gentle opening cadences of Gregory Alan Isakov's "Second Chances" filled the galerie.

It was a song he knew she was addicted to. She'd connected her iPod to the entertainment center at Castle

Bannon, and she'd played it on repeat in London as well. When he'd asked her about it, she'd told him it reminded her of love and life.

"What?!" Elizabeth laughed bringing her hands to her face as the melody filled her brain and made her hair stand on end. "Are you serious?"

She walked involuntarily towards the small table of treats. And then turned back to Connor, waiting for him to explain.

"Well, you've been so patient with everything going on at the auction house—I know I haven't been around, and I know that the security issues are making you feel uncomfortable—on top of everything else you've already had to deal with. All the insanity that comes with my life, the tabloids and . . . " his voice trailed off.

She was pretty sure he was going to bring up Sade Cantrell, but thought better of it.

Wise man.

"I just wanted to do something really special tonight. Something completely beautiful and barmy and grand."

He shoved his hands in his pockets, looking unnaturally embarrassed. It was so unlike him.

She loved when that happened.

"Too much?" his forehead creased, unsure. "It was actually Audre who helped me think of it."

Elizabeth narrowed her eyes, Audre and Connor conspiring together? She tried to wrap her brain around that conversation.

"Anyway, I decided to give you, what I believe you call . . . *the holy trifecta?*"

"Sugar, booze and dancing." Beth nodded in appreciation.

He seemed encouraged by her reaction, "And what better place to have it then at the Louvre?"

"Are we here alone?"

"Not exactly. Besides the violinist and the security guards, we also have an escort." He nodded to the other corner where a man in a suit stood in the shadows, his hands clasped in front of him.

"He's here to make sure that we don't touch the art or throw a tarte at a Da Vinci." He raised his eyebrows mischievously.

He took her hands and pulled her forward until his forehead rested against hers. "Which, if our adventures at Hogwarts are any indication of how we act around priceless treasures, I think it a very wise thing indeed." He gave her his wicked grin.

She giggled, remembering.

Elizabeth looked up into his eyes, "Sugar, booze, and dancing—that's your plan Bannon?" Her features turned grave.

Uncertainty colored his eyes.

She shook her head and put her hands on her hips. "Well it's a Damn. Fine. Plan!"

He handed her a glass of champagne. The bubbles tickled her nose. It was Cristal.

The treats she recognized from three of her favorite pâtisseries: Jacques Genin, Un Dimanche à Paris, and Café Pouchkine. All that was left. . . .

"May I have this dance?" Connor extended his hand, with a little bow.

She set her glass down and took it.

He brought her hips into him and locked their frame. Connor turned them so he could see the violinist. "A waltz, if you please."

The opening notes of Billy Joel's "Piano Man" filled the galerie. The melancholy melody rang out into the hall, filling the space with a sense of the surreal. It made her want to cry.

As they danced, Elizabeth threw her head back and watched the Masters blur in and out of view. Then she closed her eyes and let the music take them to another place complete.

The music swelled and for several minutes she existed only for each note.

Connor slowed as the song came to a beautifully sweet close. He released her and gave her a little bow, but kept his eyes on her—like that first day at the Cottage.

The violinist struck up a third tune. She laughed as she recognized the upbeat melody of Cyndi Lauper's "Girls Just Want to Have Fun". They managed a fast-paced, and slightly uneven, Viennese Waltz, laughing together as they went.

They continued in this way for several more songs until the colorful array on the table beckoned.

Connor kept one arm around her waist as she reached for an éclair and then a tarte. Playfully, she shoved a macaron in his mouth.

"There's nothing more romantic than sharing an éclair in front of Da Vinci," she mused, taking another bite.

"Speaking of which," he laced his fingers through hers, "didn't you say something about making out in front of the *Mona Lisa*?"

"Not in front of Charlie, Connor!" She lowered her voice pretending to sound shocked.

"Who's Charlie?"

She shrugged. "Our violinist," she said simply, like it was a fact.

"His name," Connor pointed, "is Benoit."

"Well I've nicknamed him Charlie," she said defiantly, staring at the man with brown hair and a French mustache.

He raised an eyebrow. "*Why?*"

She pursed her lips and nodded slowly. "I don't know, I just feel like he's a Charlie."

Connor took a sip of his champagne before setting it down on the table. He rolled his eyes, "You're mad, y'are. Did you know that? I'm in love with a lunatic."

"They say you can't help who you love," she shook her head teasing.

They made their way to the room that held the *Mona Lisa*.

Standing in front of Da Vinci's masterpiece, with only a single light illuminating her from above, was transcendent.

During the day, the golden hues were rich and warm. But with the single light they were even more so.

"I've always thought she was a bit overrated," Connor said next to her.

"*Overrated?* I disagree." She let go of his hand and took a step closer. "The first time I saw her I was seventeen. I'd heard the same thing, that she was *overrated*," she said the word with disdain, not looking at him.

"So I made sure to temper my expectations. But when I got here, even with the throngs of people all around trying to get a piece of her . . . " she sighed, "I loved her."

Connor came to stand beside her.

"Look at the warmth, the depth, the richness of it. No replica—no reproduction, has ever done it even half the justice it deserves. It's glorious."

Connor wasn't looking at *La Joconde*, he was looking down at Elizabeth, a curious half smile on his lips. "Well when you put it like that. She's a bloody masterpiece."

"That's right," Elizabeth nodded. "I'm glad you see things my way now."

"Awww, Luv." His Irish accent was thick. "I've a feelin' I'll always be made to see things your way."

He put an arm around her shoulders, "And I don't mind at'all."

In one lithe movement, he curled his arm around her neck and brought his other arm to her waist, dipping her quickly before she knew what was happening. He parted her lips in a manic sort of Hollywood kiss.

He had started it as a joke, but the kiss quickly deepened into something much stronger. Their lips tangled together, their tongues moved in knowing ways.

Elizabeth reached up and brought her arms around his neck, buried her fingers in his hair.

But the dip took her by such surprise that she hadn't been able to properly place her feet. Now the five-inch heels slipped on the smooth floor, causing her to fall backwards.

Connor tightened his arms around her just in time to catch her before she hit the floor.

They weren't quite horizontal, but Connor took the opportunity to tease her anyway, "Well this isn't *quite* what I had in mind, Lara. But if you insist, I can be prevailed upon to take off my clothes and make love to you in front of the *Mona Lisa*. It is Paris after all," he said seductively.

Gripping his arms for support, she laughed.

He gave her his most wicked grin, "Fair notice, there's a strong possibility we might get arrested. Don't worry, though, I'm sure I can get us out of it with another hefty donation."

She swatted his shoulder, "Let me up."

He hugged her to him, and shifted his weight so he could lift her. She found her footing and stood on her own.

"Well that was dramatic," she turned to him and laughed. "I guess we've made out in front of Mona now."

She drew an invisible check sign in the air, "I guess I can cross that one off of my bucket list."

He took her hand. "You have a bucket list?"

"Doesn't everyone?" she was surprised.

"Yes, I suppose so . . . is it actually written down?" he asked.

She thought for a second, "No, I guess I've jotted a few things down on, you know, a Word file or something on my laptop, but there's no *master* list."

She looked at him, curious now. "What's the top thing on your list?" she asked.

"Don't know. Never really thought about it."

"Everybody thinks about it."

"I guess I'm just peculiar then."

"You should make a list," she nodded sagely.

"If you say so, Luv." He wrapped his arm around her waist and walked her out of Room 6.

They went back for a final dance and then walked around the different galleries taking in each work at a leisurely pace.

All the main lights were turned off, with single lights illuminating each work from above and short lights emanating from below. The effect was magical and eerie.

The rooms were so quiet, she could almost hear all the way back to when the Masters had sat in their studios, in the act of creating.

She had that constant flutter in her stomach, the one she always got in old libraries—but here, the feeling was obscenely magnified. It lived somewhere between nervous and erotic.

It was delicious.

After an hour of walking closely behind Beth, viewing the art as much as he viewed her, Connor took hold of her wrist and led her towards the Richelieu Wing.

She was startled by the sudden change, the new hurried pace. "I thought we were going to go room by room!" she protested.

"*Can you go* room by room?" he asked, looking down at her feet.

Apparently, she'd started to limp a few minutes before.

Elizabeth hadn't noticed.

Damn five-inch heels.

"I didn't know we would be walking in this massive place! But I can hack it," she said defensively. "I used to be a dancer, remember?"

"Yes, your mysterious past as a dancer," he mused. "Which we still haven't gotten around to talking about."

"It's not a mysterious past, I just said it like that, that night under the stars in Ireland to pique your interest."

"OK," he laughed. He raised an eyebrow, "Well, it worked."

"Good, because there's lots that you still don't know about me Mr. Bannon."

"Is that right, Miss Lara? I look forward to uncovering all of your secrets." His eyes glinted with the light from the nearest painting.

"OK, so where are we going?" He was pulling her too quickly. It was getting more difficult to ignore the pain.

His voice shook a degree, a level of anxiety broke through. "Cutting to the chase, Luv."

Suddenly, Elizabeth felt nervous, nauseated. A strange sort of angst crept up and spread throughout her body. What else had he planned?

They reached La Galerie Michel-Ange, passing several extraordinary Italian sculptures. The galerie was based on the Salle des Caryatides and housed part of the museum's Italian sculpture collection.

He brought her to Room 4 of the Michelangelo Gallery, next to the Cour Marly and its glass roof.

And then he stopped.

All the lights in this room were turned off. Even the security lights.

She took a step forward, bringing him with her. "What's . . .?"

She examined the room, her eyes adjusted. Room 4 had a row of large windows that looked out onto the Cour Marly.

The moon was nearly full and directly overhead, which meant that the Cour was filled to the brim with moonlight that spilled through the windows and into all of the adjacent rooms, including 4, lighting the white sculptures and basking them in a lavender glow.

She released his hand and walked towards the sculpture he had intended. The one she forgot was there.

"Oh wow . . . I didn't, I mean I had forgotten . . . " she said under her breath.

"When was the last time you were here?" Connor came up behind her.

"I don't know," she shook her head. "I've been to Paris several times obviously, but I haven't come to the Louvre in, maybe, *twelve* years? I do all of the other museums regularly, Rodin, Musée d'Orsay . . . because I love them and because I know how long I like to spend in each."

She paused, thinking. "But the Louvre is always so massive, and the tourists . . . so I tend to shy away from it."

She closed the distance walking all the way up to the short one-foot-tall metal barrier.

Psyche Revived by Cupid's Kiss was nothing short of spectacular in the moonlight.

The artist, Canova, had taken his inspiration from the legend as recounted by the Latin author, Apuleius.

In the legend, Cupid falls in love with the beautiful Psyche. His mother Venus, jealous of her beauty sends him to shoot her with an arrow so that she might fall in love with an awful man.

Instead, Cupid sees her and falls desperately in love. He secretly marries the mortal woman, never letting her see him. Each night he went to her room and made love to her, but forbade her from seeing his face.

Until one night, spurred by the negative suspicions of her sisters that Psyche had married a monster, she sneaks into her husband's room and is so shocked to see lovely Cupid, that she accidentally spills hot wax on him. Cupid wakes and leaves her, hurt by her betrayal.

Desperate to find her husband, she goes to Venus who forces her to undergo a series of trials, the last of which causes her to fall into a deathly sleep. Cupid revives her and the gods bless their marriage, giving Psyche ambrosia and making her the goddess of the Soul.

The marble sculpture depicted the moment of Psyche's revival; her arms stretched up behind her in a very balletic movement, she arches her back and cranes her neck so that her beloved Cupid might kiss her lips. Cupid leans down with his wings extended, his right leg braced against a rock as he lifts her, cupping one breast in his palm protectively.

For several moments, Elizabeth forgot where she was. She forgot that Connor was standing next to her. Time and space ceased to exist as she connected with something outside of herself.

Something from the Universe.

The work took her breath away. Even though she'd spent many waking hours staring at replicas and sketches of Canova's work, the sculpture itself, and seeing it in this way with just the moonlight, moved her more than any single work of art had ever done.

A single tear trailed down her cheek. She only had eyes for the statue. She didn't even notice when Connor used his index finger to trace the tear back to her eye.

He stayed silent, letting her have this moment, gratified that his surprise had moved her so completely. But he was nervous, as well. Because it was nearly time to brave the main event and he had no idea how she would react.

He knew it was a gamble. But it was one he had to take. She had bewitched him, she owned his body and his soul—and he needed to tell her so, even if she wasn't ready to hear it.

Elizabeth revived, bringing her hand to her face wiping the remaining moisture away. Without looking at Connor she took his hand and brought it in front of her, so she could hold it in both of hers.

"Thank you," she whispered. "As long as I live, I will never forget this."

"I'm glad you like it, Lara . . . " his voice trailed off. The time was now, before he lost his nerve. "There's actually another reason I brought you here."

She looked up at him now, finding his face.

Without another word he took both of her hands in his and dropped down to one knee.

Elizabeth's breath caught in her throat. The moonlight illuminated his blue eyes, his face, his white shirt.

"Elizabeth Lara, I know that you don't believe that people should be in relationships to save each other, but you saved me that afternoon when you walked in on me in the nip. You saved me with your smile, with your odd little ways, with the way you forged an unknown path after life dealt you so much grief.

"You brought me back to life after my mother died. You helped me be a better man, to see the world in a way that seems almost magical, unreal even. And I hope that I helped save you a little along the way.

"I want to wake up to you every day of my life, I want to hold you in my arms every night until we're both old and gray. You're it for me, Luv. You own me body and soul, and I know that this is a very risky thing to do—seeing as we've only been back together for a few weeks—and I know that you usually need some sort of list that helps you analyze every aspect of a situation, and I know that you're probably going to say no.

"But I don't care, I can't go another day without asking you to be mine, without telling you that I'm yours. *Forever*.

"So what I'm saying, Lara, is that it's OK if you say no tonight because I will just keep asking until you say yes. Because I know, and I've always known, that you and I are meant to be. We make each other laugh, we make each other better.

"So . . ." he took a deep breath, "how about it, Lara? Will you consent to a life of love and adventure? Will you marry me?"

At some point during his speech she'd stopped breathing. The same vacuum that had existed when she had gazed upon Psyche and her Cupid had sucked all the air out of the room as soon as he'd gone down on one knee and she had realized what *cutting to the chase* really meant.

Her first thought was: *this is insane*. But as he continued to talk, as she continued to see the sincerity and honesty and love in his face, she fell further from her head until she was firmly rooted in her heart.

As he knelt in front of her, she couldn't hear or see anything beyond his blue eyes. Sensing that this was one of those key moments in life, she desperately tried to think through what was happening, to access her analytical brain, but she couldn't.

Suddenly, there was nothing more logical or real than the man kneeling in front of her. In spite of the battlefield of crumpled marriages she had witnessed, none of it mattered. Once he had asked, it wasn't even a choice.

But as she opened her mouth, she still wasn't sure which part of her would win out . . . her head . . . or her heart.

Connor looked up at her for an agonizing minute, desperately trying to convey how much love he had for her in his eyes; how he would never let her down; how he would always be there to hold her hand, to dance with her, to feed her chocolate.

Finally, Elizabeth found her voice. She drew her eyebrows together and filled her lungs with air. "Yes," she whispered. It was so low she wasn't sure she'd actually said it.

"Yes," she said it again more firmly.

Connor's face split into an earth-shattering grin. The Holy Grail of Christmas morning smiles. He took a very large, princess cut diamond ring from his pocket and placed it on her finger.

Then he lifted her in his arms, circling around so that her feet fanned out in the air behind her.

Their laughter filled the Michelangelo Gallery as he spun them in place. His eyes sparkled with the moonlight as he set her down.

And there, under the watchful eye of Cupid and his Psyche, they sealed it with a kiss.

Chapter 9: Restless Security

"So you realize you've just agreed to marry me, right? That means you're stuck with me *forever*." His eyes grew wide at the forever part, teasing.

"Ohhh . . . is that what just happened? Well then, is it too late to change my mind?" she poked his ribs playfully.

It was after midnight, they were back in the car.

He took her hand and brought it into his lap, "Are you ready for that?" he asked.

She tilted her head, "Are you *trying* to talk me out of it?"

"No, definitely not. I'm over the moon, I'm just having some trouble believin' it. I thought you were going to refuse me—which I was prepared for, because I knew that eventually you would say yes. But for you to say yes tonight?" His smile grew exponentially. His glee was palpable.

"I hope I didn't disappoint you by accepting on your first try?!" She bit the inside of her lip to keep from smiling.

"No, no, Luv, on the contrary," he drew her close until she was practically sitting in his lap. "No man could be happier."

They kissed then slow and sweet, relishing in their newfound commitment to one another. It was a level of happy Beth didn't know could exist.

This man wanted to spend the rest of his living days with her. All the marriage and divorce and property settlement bullshit aside, there was something poetic, even magical about that.

Several minutes later, they emerged hand-in-hand from the elevator, laughing together like a couple of teenagers. Tipsy from the champagne, high on their new relationship status.

Connor wrapped his arms around her waist and leaned in for a kiss before extracting the keys from inside his pocket.

He inserted the key in the lock and then suddenly threw his arm out placing her behind him.

She was on high alert in an instant. Braced for whatever was happening.

"What's wrong?"

"The door is unlocked," he whispered.

She exhaled. With the way he'd reacted she'd thought they were under some sort of attack. "Oh well, maybe you were just so taken by my dress that you forgot to lock it on our way out," she said in a normal voice, returning to her engagement high.

His head snapped back, his eyes wide, he threw her a look of warning.

Fear and anxiety were now radiating from his body. It instantly wiped the smile from her face. His reaction was scaring her.

The last time she'd seen him like this a man was standing in the cottage pointing a gun at her.

If someone had broken into the apartment with the intention of doing physical harm, wouldn't they have locked the door and then waited to trap them?

Connor shifted the keys in his hand until he was holding something other else. She looked over his shoulder at his hand.

"What is that?" she whispered.

"It's a SwissMiniGun."

She looked closer, it looked like it was attached to his keys.

"You have a gun on your key chain?" she was dumbfounded. "You proposed with a gun in your pocket?" Her voice had returned to normal.

He hushed her, "Lara!" he whispered in warning.

He opened the door carefully keeping Beth behind him, the tiny two-inch gun barely stuck out of his hand, it looked like a toy.

"Can that thing even penetrate skin?" she whispered, clutching the back of his blazer.

"There's some debate about that," he whispered impatiently back and shot her one final look of warning.

The apartment was dead silent. Elizabeth's eyes darted here and there covering the space, trying to find their intruder.

Nothing seemed out of place, except for a piece of paper on the floor by the apartment phone they'd just installed. It could have been knocked to the floor by an intruder or a simple breeze.

Beth straightened out of the crouched position she had assumed. Quietly she took off her five-inch heels so she could step forward without making any noise.

But instead of walking farther into the apartment, Connor stepped backwards pushing her with his body back out the door, and locking it behind him.

He kept the gun in his right hand and fished the phone out of his pocket with his left. Quickly, he dialed a number.

"I need you up here now. Call in the team." His voice was strained, the veins in his neck were throbbing.

He grabbed Beth by the wrist and dragged her back down the hall and into the elevator. She was still carrying her shoes, but they dropped out of her hand as he pulled her more urgently.

When they reached the foyer inside the door that led to Rue Servandoni, he picked her up and carried her out to the street and back into the car, getting in next to her. She watched as three men, one in slacks and a dress shirt and two in sleek security suits, unlocked the red front door to the building and went inside.

She'd never seen any of them before, except for the man in slacks and a shirt. He was her plain clothes bodyguard. She had no idea when he had hired a full security team, or what they were expected to do.

She sat back against the smooth black leather of the town car. Looking out the window across the street to the Luxembourg Gardens.

She felt a familiar uneasiness, a sense of being out of control. The last time she had felt this nervous fluttering in her stomach—that didn't remotely resemble excited butterflies—she'd been standing in the middle of the village in Ireland, reading a tabloid.

It had shown her, for the first time, that Connor's life was a much bigger pond than it felt like when it was just the two of them.

She remembered how she'd thought then that she wasn't sure what she'd gotten herself into. Now more than ever that seemed to be true.

She turned to him, "Connor, tell me the truth." She was dead serious. "Are you into anything illegal, the mob or whatever the Irish or European version of the mob is? Because someone is out to get you or it seems that way, and I just don't think that some twenty-something kid who I embarrassed, and then who, *granted*," she raised her palms, making the allowance, "held me at gunpoint, would do this. Why? For what reason—it doesn't make any sense."

She let the words out in a rush, giving into the stream of consciousness talking that she was prone to when she was nervous, frustrated, and felt out of control.

"No, Lara. I told you I'm not into anything illegal," he shook his head in frustration. Of all the nights . . . they'd been so happy mere moments before and now this. "But when you have this much money, when the press has built you up as this *identity*, that life—whether I wanted it or not—makes me a high profile target for all kinds of people."

He sighed, "I've always had a security team, there's always some level of security involved in my life." He'd hoped to ease her into this part gradually. It wasn't ideal, but he felt the constant need to divulge the more difficult areas of his life one at a time so as not to scare her off.

Beth thought back to their time in Ireland, when it had been just the two of them. "What about Castle Bannon?"

"Well what you don't realize is that Castle Bannon is practically a fortress and Declan's former military. So even though you didn't see any security, we were always surrounded by some protection.

"I've taken on some additional personal security, like your bodyguard Alain. I've also hired a security consultant to help figure out what's going on at the auction house; to go through what we know so far and analyze what's been happening, and why it's happening."

Connor gritted his teeth and clenched his jaw, concentrating his frustration in his face. It had been a wonderful night and he'd wanted it to keep going. She made him feel like his life could be almost normal, this latest incident was a rude awakening.

He knew all the extra security weighed on her. He wondered if in the end it would all be too much for her. If his life would be too much.

She thought through everything that she knew so far about the breaches in security. It just didn't add up—unless he was keeping something from her. Which, considering their history, was highly possible.

She turned on him, bringing her bare feet underneath her, "Connor, you need to tell me what's going on. I can tell that you're keeping something from me—actual events or just suspicions, I can't tell. But, the point is that I don't think I have all the information.

"And considering that you just asked me to spend the rest of my life with you and I said *yes,*" she looked at him pointedly, "I think it's time you started treating me like a partner."

Her eyes were grave as she said the next part, "Because if you think for one second that I'm going to continue down this path with you not knowing everything that's going on, *when* it happens, I may as well just go upstairs and pack my things when the security team clears out." It would hurt like hell, tear out her insides, but she would do it. She'd wasted too much of her life living blindly . . . and the truth was too important.

He let out a deep sigh and ran his fingers through his hair. He searched her face, the way he sometimes did before deciding on a course of action.

"OK, first let me set something straight. I haven't kept any of this from you on purpose. I just don't know how to handle these things with someone by my side. Like you, I'm used to acting alone, working things out on my own, so maybe I have a few walls that I need to work through, as well.

"When I was in London," he continued, "someone broke into my hotel room at the Ritz. I still don't know why. It was about that time that I left London after telling you everything I had done and all that I felt. I had to check on the auction house and the apartment, make sure they were both secure. I also thought I should give you some time and space. Being in a different country seemed like the best way to accomplish that since I wasn't sure how I would get through the next few days without showing up like a lost puppy at your door.

"Even though things were up in the air with us, somehow I knew that we would figure it out together, so I made sure that the decorations reflected your taste—you already know that I took some extreme measures to make that happen—"

She motioned with her hand, a simple wave signaling him to move on.

"OK, then there were the phone calls. Some days they were incessant, tying up the line, and never leaving a message, never saying anything. And there was that break-in where someone smashed a window, and the break-in that happened the other night, and now there's this."

He stopped talking. She couldn't tell if he was finished.

"Is that it?"

He didn't answer her.

"Is there more or do you have suspicions that you're reluctant to share with the class?"

His lips set in a line. "It's the latter."

"Fine, tell me," she said impatiently.

"I think that perhaps . . ." he hesitated, "that incident with the maggot who tried to drug you in London wasn't random. I think you were targeted because of me."

His words sent chills down her spine, even though she knew it was impossible. She'd chosen that pub at random.

"That seems highly unlikely." She thought through it all. He was being paranoid. "All of these break-ins they are directed at you, not me," she said more to herself than him, trying to find the missing piece, put the puzzle together.

She narrowed her eyes, thinking. "Tell me why you think that Stephen's behind it all?"

He sighed, considering.

"I mean if you think it's Stephen, why would he hire some guy named Jeff to drug me at a bar in London? Why would he be breaking into all of these places that you are connected to and taking noth--"

Connor cut her off, "I don't know that it is Stephen!" He waved his hands in a frustrated gesture, cornered by her barrage.

"I just—I know that these security breaches are connected to me, but I can't shake this gut feeling that they are directed at you as well. And if they're directed at you, then it *has* to be Stephen."

Then another thought struck him as he looked at her, lips twitching up a degree, "Or have you ticked off any other people on the continent that I don't know about?"

She rested her head against the seat, thinking. She mostly kept to herself, and had only spent time with her friends.

She shook her head, "No there's no one."

And then something else occurred to her, "What about Stephen's father? Didn't you say that he's some bigwig in Cork?"

Connor shook his head, "Yes he is, but he's the sort that would cut his son off and distance himself from the situation—which is exactly what he did. To wade back in now and take me on?

"No, it would only further his exposure. Plus, this level of harassment is unfocused, petty. It doesn't reek of some grand design."

She turned her body so she could look back out the window towards Luxembourg, her voice grew soft. "No, I suppose it doesn't."

Twenty minutes later, they were safely installed in the apartment. Nothing had been taken, nothing was out of place. Connor, made it a point to tell her everything the security team did. Which, apparently included sweeping for bugs and surveillance equipment.

She went to bed that night feeling uneasy. *Surveillance equipment?*

Somehow, in all the excitement and love and lust and sugar and booze, she had forgotten that Connor's life involved so much more than just the two of them.

She curled up on her side while Connor wrapped his arms around her, nestling his head into her neck, "I love you Lara. I can't wait to start a life with you," he whispered drowsily.

She drew his arms around her more tightly and fell into a restless sleep.

CHAPTER 10: DINNER IN MÉRÉ

"Santé!" They all clinked glasses.

The family dinner party in Méré at Château Fleury was well underway.

They were already into their sixth bottle of wine, and she and Connor had only been at the château for an hour.

They were gathered around a large table outside. In a space that was like a porch, if porches had a full roof, concrete floors, and classic eighteenth century French arches. *And overlooked several acres of manicured gardens.*

It was a gorgeous night; the family had prepared a feast to welcome them even though it was a small party of eight. It was just Matthieu, Alexandre, Emily and Emily's three daughters—all slender framed beauties with dark hair.

The eldest Liliane was thirty-eight and married with two children, Ava and Bastien, who were with their father for the weekend.

Renée the middle daughter, was an architect living in Paris and was about Elizabeth's age at thirty-six.

The youngest of the three, Bridgett had a different father than Liliane and Renée. She was thirty-two and lived in Paris. She was by far the most French of the three.

"It is terrible," Bridgett continued to go on, pressing three fingers together and waving them at the table for emphasis.

Her French accent was thick. It appeared to Elizabeth that she was actually quite capable of speaking without the accent, but chose instead to draw it out. To prove her Frenchness. "They just bring them in from these large factories. All croissants should be made fresh and with real butter."

Renée chimed in, "Bridgett, if it were up to you every croissant would be made fresh, on-site, with a side of cynicism to spread on top."

They all laughed.

Bridgett crossed her arms, pouting and leaned back in her chair. "This is Paris! That used to mean something, now it is all becoming like America! The burgers, the fast food. . . ."

Elizabeth smiled at her cousin, grateful that no one was putting on a pretense for her sake. All of them were exactly who they were and nothing or no one was going to change that.

Her aunt Emily was very sweet and gazed at her face often. Apparently, she had been good friends with Carolina during the several months that she had spent here. Now in her sixties, she had retired after working almost forty years at a bank in Paris.

Matthieu was exactly as he had been at Musée Rodin and the apartment. Very genuine, very sweet, and he continued to feel more British than French. He didn't seem to possess that same sense of cynicism that Beth had so often observed in the French. Bridgett was Exhibit A.

Matthieu was a true idealist. The more she knew him, the easier it was to understand why he had been the love of Mags' life.

He possessed a pure soul, capable of only seeing the best in people, and no major life punch in the gut was going to change that.

She loved him already.

Alexandre seemed rather quiet amongst his family. It surprised her since he seemed so at home in the public eye and at his show, easily falling into conversation, welcoming people and showing them his work.

Renée, who was sitting on her right, confirmed it quietly while everyone else was lost in their own separate conversations. "Yes, out in the world, when he needs to be he can be loud and boisterous, eccentric—what you would expect an artist to be. But here he's usually quiet and thoughtful."

And then Renée gave her a sidelong glance and a smile, "But sometimes, he stalks off for no reason."

Her father looked at her often, she tried not to notice, but it seemed that his eyes rarely left her face.

It was as if her presence, her features reminded him of something, some memory or previous life. From what she could tell, the revelation that he had a daughter, had made him very happy.

Matthieu had made sure to tell her as soon as they'd arrived. "He's been prancing around this place on cloud nine, singing and hugging everyone and smiling much too often—it was alarming I tell you, Lizzie."

Her cousins had all been filled in on the events that had transpired that week. Liliane and Renée were gratified, delighted in their new friend and cousin.

Bridgett seemed ambivalent, like it was to be expected that an unknown daughter of Alexandre or any man really would suddenly turn up. It seemed that nothing could phase her.

"Don't mind Bridgett, she's been drinking her coffee black, like her heart since she was ten," Renée told Beth.

Bridgett was sitting directly across from them, "Putain," she said under her breath, staring daggers at Renée.

Renée narrowed her eyes and shook her head in response, and then they both laughed together.

It was a strange thing to behold, that way siblings interacted with each other. One moment they were saying nasty things to each other, and then somehow, without saying anything else, they could laugh together.

She enjoyed them.

Wherever possible, Connor kept hold of her hand. They shared little looks together when someone said something funny or outlandish, which happened quite often around the table. It seemed no subject was off-limits over wine and dinner in France.

They'd already discussed Liliane's marriage woes with her husband of twelve years, Valentin.

And Bridgett's ongoing and very lively sexcapades. And they talked about how Renée and her partner Nicolle were trying to have a baby.

Elizabeth was so glad that everyone was being themselves, airing everything out, not holding anything back. It was a relief not to have to go through all the awkward politeness.

It was still unclear just how close she would end up being with her family, but she was glad to know that things could be easy between them.

Bridgett looked at Elizabeth, "What does the future 'old for you now that you have located Matthieu and delivered your message?" she asked directly. "Are you staying together or Connor are you going back to Ireland?"

Bridgett didn't believe in relationships or monogamy.

Elizabeth and Connor looked at each other, with Elizabeth answering, "We haven't talked about that yet, really."

Connor gave her a small smile, she could see him daring her with his eyes. He wanted her to tell them about the engagement.

"Definitely staying together," she smiled at the table, "in fact, yesterday . . ." she hesitated, recognizing the feeling rising up inside her as a mild form of terror, which only worked to make up her mind. "We got engaged," she finished, trying to look only pleased and not shocked by the words coming out of her own mouth. It would take some getting used to.

And she hadn't yet processed the break-in or what it all meant, the life she was signing up for. And that nagging thought she kept running from . . . that commitment would mean a loss of freedom; not to mention the bodyguards and surveillance equipment.

She'd comforted herself with the idea of a long engagement. There would be plenty of time to figure it out, discuss the details.

The table erupted in congratulations and cheers all over again.

Renée grabbed her hand, "But where is your ring?" she asked.

Elizabeth had forgotten to put it on, or at least that was what she'd told the table. Wearing the ring would make it real. She was acutely aware of her conflicting emotions. She'd said yes, but she was having a difficult time not having one foot out the door.

She didn't have the chance to answer before Liliane asked, "Where did he propose?"

"At the Louvre," Elizabeth answered.

Bridgett made a face of disgust, "Oh that place is 'orrible, just 'orrible," she complained.

Instead of feeling offended, Elizabeth smiled. Her new cousin and her propensity to be negative and complain about everything, was starting to be very amusing indeed.

Like a French caricature. A Parisian dressed all in black smoking with one hand, strong dark espresso in the other, going on about how the Eiffel Tower was *'ideous* and the Louvre was *'ideous* and Da Vinci was an *ideeut* and generally going on about everything that was bad in the world.

"Oh I don't know," Beth smiled wide at her cousin. "It was rather poetic, *magical,* even." Her eyes grew wide at the word magical, daring her cousin to disagree with her.

Bridgett's eyes narrowed and her face softened, "I like you," she pointed at Beth with her wine glass hand. "You cut through the bullshit," she said taking a sip.

Everyone at the table was stunned into silence.

Liliane spoke, "Wow Elizabeth that's high praise. Bridgett doesn't like anyone."

They all laughed.

Bridgett turned her attention to Connor, "So Connor was it true about you and that Sade?"

Wow, she really didn't pull any punches. Elizabeth stopped moving, bracing herself for whatever he would say.

"No, Bridgett," he said firmly. "It was actually a ploy I devised to make Elizabeth jealous."

Beth looked over at him. His expression was all mischief.

She narrowed her eyes and waited for him to finish.

"You see," he leaned forward to include them in the conspiracy. "When we were together in Ireland she was very much the cool character. I was already head over heels, but

153

this one," he took a glance at Elizabeth. "She was ready to leave me and move on to the next.

"And Sade, as you know, had just broken up with Chase, so she agreed to kiss me in front of the photogs.

"And sure enough Elizabeth saw it back in London and, *jealous* with rage, she pursued me until I relented." He let his Irish storytelling flair take over.

Elizabeth's mouth dropped open as she watched him build the story.

She turned to the table, quickly composing herself. "Actually I was seeing Wes Cartwright in London when he came over to profess his love for me."

She leaned into her audience, bringing her family into her conspiracy now, "He groveled." She drew her eyebrows together, nodding like it was pathetic. "It wasn't pretty," she shook her head.

Everyone at the table looked between Connor and Elizabeth and back again, not sure who to believe.

The pair looked at each other with big smiles and then burst into laughter. They leaned into each other and kissed quickly before turning back to the table and telling them the real story.

Elizabeth was relieved that they could work together in that way, easily; even joke about their past issues.

It felt like a good sign.

"When is the wedding?" Liliane asked.

"Oh not for a very long time." "Very soon, I hope." Elizabeth and Connor declared at the same time.

They looked at each other, surprised by the others' response.

Everyone looked down at their plates, politely giving them a second.

Elizabeth looked up at them, "It's clearly very new," she smiled.

Connor reached over and squeezed her hand giving her a wink, making it feel less awkward.

Maybe they didn't have all the answers, but they would figure it out, *together.*

She smiled back.

"And what's this?" Alexandre said in French, bringing everyone's attention to him. "Did you not think to ask the father? Is it not traditional?" He moved his hands in the air dramatically. His face was serious as stone.

Everyone stared blankly.

The awkward seconds ticked by.

Then his face split into a big grin, quickly followed by a chuckle. Then he threw his head back and howled, a boisterous laugh that reminded Elizabeth of Gérard Depardieu.

He slapped the table shaking the cutlery.

After an awkward moment, everyone understood that he'd been joking and joined in the laughter.

Alexandre rose and walked over to Elizabeth. He took her hand and kissed it, "Congratulations," he said in English, nodding.

"Thank you."

It was a small gesture, but it felt so big to her. She had a fiancé and a father, and an aunt, and a great-uncle, and three cousins. What a wonderfully bizarre journey Mags had sent her on.

Alexandre released her and returned to his seat.

The others began talking amongst themselves laughing here and there as Elizabeth took a sip of her wine. Her eyes watered, she was overwhelmed with all the people and love and family that had found their way into her life.

It was a far cry from the day when she had sprinted into Kensington Park, and cried out into the tree grove as the rain pummeled her from above.

Thinking that she was alone in the world.

Connor took her hand and leaned in to kiss her neck. "That's right Lara, you're not alone."

She looked up into his blue eyes, and for a moment it was just the two of them. She smiled as he rested his forehead against hers.

"So your Magdalen left you a château in Millemont?" Renée asked, sometime later.

"That's less than ten miles from here," Emily observed.

Beth glanced at Matthieu who was listening with a sad smile.

Bridgett chimed in, "It's too bad that she never came. Matthieu was very much in love with her. I remember when we were children it was always my Lena this and my Lena that."

Again Elizabeth looked to Matthieu who had turned bright red.

Everyone else stopped their individual conversations to listen.

Matthieu rested his hands on the table, "That's right my children, some would call it a sad love story. But it does not do to live with regret. Magdalen always said that the only true sin in this world was to deny what was in your heart. Not just to deny your love for someone else, but to not listen to your heart when it calls you to do something or go somewhere. To follow your path. I believe she always stayed true to that."

He glanced down at his hands again thinking. "I will say this," his eyes watered, "I would have loved to share my life with her. What an adventure that would have been."

And with that he raised his glass, "To Love, my children. May you always have it and give it freely."

"Santé," they clinked glasses.

By three in the morning each person had had their own food and drink induced heart-to-heart with virtually every other person on the patio.

There were pictures and stories and things families shared. Emily showed her pictures of the girls as children, and even some pictures of Carolina's time in France. One was identical to the picture that Mags had left for her.

The one Beth wished her great-aunt had explained, left her the names of the people in the picture. It turned out to be

Carolina, Mags, and Emily was the other female in the picture. The two men were Matthieu and Alexandre.

Another mystery solved.

When they were set to leave, Liliane invited them to stay the night.

The château had seven bedrooms, three of which were master bedroom suites. The other four were also comfortably large.

They were all planning to stay the night.

She was about to accept when Connor stepped in, "Thank you for the offer, that's lovely, but we have a driver. It'll be a breeze to get back to Paris and our apartment."

Liliane nodded, understanding.

Elizabeth interjected, "Actually, I'd like to stay."

She quickly became enamored with the idea of having a sleepover with her cousins, who clearly showed no sign of slowing down.

They'd already grabbed a few more bottles and were in the kitchen stocking up on provisions to take upstairs.

Elizabeth had started to walk into the house after them, when Connor grabbed her arm and stopped her.

"Elizabeth?" Connor gave her a tight smile.

Emily and Liliane picked up on his tone, "We'll give you a moment," they said. "We'll be in the kitchen."

"What's wrong?" she asked him, pleasantly tipsy. He looked delicious.

"Lara, it's too dangerous," he said firmly. "You're exposed out here, there's no security from what I can tell, it's just wide open."

His words had no effect on her, "What do you mean? What's going to happen out here? I want to stay—it'll be fine. You can go back, you can just send the driver back for me in the morning or I can find another way to Paris," she said to him, completely carefree.

"Lara," he said more firmly.

She stopped smiling and took in the anger that was starting to transform his features. He didn't look as delicious anymore.

"It's too dangerous," he said again, a strange sort of red started to rise up his neck.

She put her hands on her hips, "What are you talking about? That's insane, don't be ridiculous; it'll be fine. If you're so worried just stay with me." She wrapped her arms around his waist and kissed his neck.

He grabbed her arms and placed her in front of him.

He took out his phone, shaking his head. "If you want to stay, I'll have to call the security team out here and it's past three in the morning."

"So don't call them." She crossed her arms. Now angry with him for ruining the moment.

She finally had a family to spend time with, and the château was beautiful and large and historic.

And the village of Méré was quiet and sleepy and quaint. There was nothing to worry about.

"You're being paranoid," she snapped.

"No, I'm being careful. You mean too much to me, Lara. I can't risk it."

"OK, well . . . I'm nice and tipsy right now. I love you and you can go back to Paris," she waved her arm in the general direction of the city. "But I'm staying here," she gave him a smile, trying to change his mood.

"OK?" She tried to sound carefree. She went up on her tiptoes to give him a peck. Again he grabbed her arms, this time he held her in place. "Lara, you're not staying and *that's final,*" he said forcefully into her face.

Those words. Her stomach dropped to her feet. Instantly, she stumbled back, out of his arms.

"Excuse me?" Her voice rose. The cool night did nothing to keep her from fuming.

"Let me be clear." She paused to take a breath. "No matter how much I love you and how much you love me, you will *never* have the right to restrict my movements or actions— even if it is out of concern for my safety."

She stared daggers at him, "*Got it?*" she finished, shaking with anger.

He narrowed his eyes, this time not backing down. "Oh, I've got it," he nodded. "I've got no say in your safety, no right to ensure that the woman I love is protected, is that it? I thought we were beyond this—you're shutting me out."

"In my safety?" she turned the words over in her mouth. It was absurd. "Because I want to sleep in a house with my cousins and stay up talking about . . . I don't know, what do grown women talk about at a sleepover? I haven't had a slumber party since I was ten," she waved her arms around dramatically.

"You're right Connor; this is me shutting you out, me being reckless with my own life, that's exactly what this is!" She was livid.

"Elizabeth!" he snapped. "This is serious!"

The blood rose to his face, he was seething. "This life with me, security issues will happen, and you're going to have to listen to me. Because I can't lose you," he said it with some amount of vulnerability, but mostly he was angry with her.

Angry for not letting him in, angry for not seeing the truth in his words, how exposed the property was.

The blood rose to her face as well. They were fuming at the same temperature; on opposite sides with no bridge in sight. She straightened, "I love you, but you need to go back to the apartment now," she said with a quiet firmness that signaled she was done. "I will be fine."

The muscles in his face throbbed. The veins in his neck popped.

Without another word he stalked out of the patio and into the house. She followed slowly, listening as he excused himself with a convincingly pleasant goodbye; he thanked them for their hospitality.

And then he was gone.

CHAPTER 11: THE DOWNPOUR

Beth ended up staying at Château Fleury through Wednesday; her family did the same.

Liliane came and went as she needed to tend to her children Ava and Bastien. But Renée and Bridgett took a few days off from work. Emily lived in a nice house just up the road, but even she slept at the château.

Elizabeth didn't have anything with her, but with three female cousins of similar ages, any problems she might have had resolved themselves quickly.

They took care of her without a second thought, dressing her in clothes that fit perfectly, and were effortlessly chic.

The lady who took care of the château a woman called, Madame Maro, was sent out to get basic toiletries from the village store.

It would have been easy to pop into Paris and pack a bag of her things, but Elizabeth enjoyed the sense of freedom she was experiencing in Méré. She took great comfort in the fact that not everything had to be perfect.

She didn't need her toothbrush or her favorite makeup or even her clothes, she just needed to keep living in this time and place where she had a family and they were as eager to know her as she was to know them.

They had long three hour lunches and even longer five hour dinners. Matthieu and Alexandre were as present as the women. All of them taking the time to sit together and drink and look at pictures and tell stories.

They walked to the village several times. Her cousins introduced her eagerly to the postmistress and to the local business owners, and anyone walking down the street.

Even Bridgett seemed happy-*ish*, less quick to complain about whatever was bothering her in that moment.

It would have been perfect, if the Connor fight hadn't been left hanging in the air, somewhere in the back of her brain.

It felt wrong, to not be on good terms.

Neither of them had called or left messages. She would've been more alarmed, if not for the glimpses she caught of the plain clothes bodyguard, who followed at a distance anytime they went out into the village.

No matter how angry he was with her, he refused to leave her unprotected.

And so Elizabeth settled in nicely with her family, having three almost perfect days. She felt like a giddy five-year-old, a ten-year-old, a sixteen-year-old, going through the stages of life all over again with a new set of people.

And hearing about how they had weathered life so far.

They'd gone from speaking in English for Elizabeth's benefit since she'd found it difficult to keep up with their blazing French initially, to speaking almost exclusively in their native tongue. The more time she spent with them, the easier it was to decipher what they were all saying.

Matthieu was the exception; he'd spent so many decades teaching in the UK that he seemed to prefer speaking with her in English. The two of them spoke about Mags so regularly that it almost felt like even she was staying at the château with them.

Elizabeth enjoyed getting to know her great-aunt better; seeing her through someone else's eyes. She'd been able to ask Matthieu about so many things; what she was like with him . . . what she was like in her youth . . . how she had changed over the years. Elizabeth listened attentively to each story, like a child.

She'd especially enjoyed hearing about their time in Verneuil-sur-Avre.

"Matthieu what happened after that incident with the butcher? Did Mags lose her access to meat?" Elizabeth asked Matthieu one night when the others had been busy talking amongst themselves.

"Certainly not!" he answered with a mischievous smile, as he remembered the way he'd met Magdalen.

He didn't continue.

Beth prodded, "Well, did the butcher apologize?"

"No," Matthieu mused, "he was much too hard a man for that."

He was in no hurry to offer an explanation, having too much fun losing himself in the memory.

Elizabeth's eyes went wide impatiently as she gave her great-uncle an expression he already recognized as her *well then out with it* look. She waved her hands for emphasis.

He chuckled, gratified they'd been able to build a comfortable relationship so quickly. "You are impatient, aren't you, Lizzie?" His eyes twinkled.

"Only most of the time," she smiled.

"Can't a man enjoy a good memory at his own pace?"

Beth didn't skip a beat, "Of course, unless said man is holding the cherished memory hostage from his doting niece who is most anxious to share in it with him."

"All right then, I'll oblige you." He leaned forward in his chair on the patio while his eyes remained trained on the space in front of him, like he was watching the memory on a screen.

"Mags did not lose her access to meat because she marched into the butcher's the very next day, defiant as ever. She wore an expression . . ." he shot Beth a quick half smile and for a moment Elizabeth could imagine what he must have looked like as a young man. "I'll never forget it, she held her head high and stared him directly in the eyes without blinking, daring him to refuse her."

Beth laughed. She could see it as clearly as if she was inside Matthieu's head reliving it with him.

Her great-uncle continued, "He didn't, of course, and after a few weeks he even came to give her extra as an apology for almost hitting her and yelling at Michelle. All of the townspeople were curt with him, not rude, just short—went

166

about their business as quickly as possible while in the shop; responded only with the briefest of greetings on the street . . . that sort of thing."

He looked at her then, his expression evolved from amusement to appreciation. "He changed after that—he was never a joyous man, but he became tolerable. Lena had that ability, I always admired her for it; she could drive people to change."

Beth's face split into an instant grin; she was acutely aware of her great-aunt's ability.

Matthieu leaned over and patted her on the arm as the silence grew and they lost themselves in their own memories of the woman they both loved.

On Wednesday afternoon she texted Connor, saying that she was ready to go back to Paris. He responded with a simple text: *Bertrand will be there in an hour.*

"À bientôt!" Her cousins said in turn, kissing her three times. Emily, Alexandre, and Matthieu all kissed her and then hugged her fiercely, none more so than Matthieu.

Elizabeth looked at her family through the back window of the town car as they stood in front of the château waving. She didn't turn around again until Bertrand pulled onto the main lane and the house disappeared from view.

She made eye contact with Bertrand through the rearview mirror. "Thank you for coming."

He nodded. "Of course, Mademoiselle," he said with a thick French accent.

She let her eyes focus on the rolling green hills and vineyards out the window. There were tall trees and small cliffs in the distance, the landscape was old and varied; the area even played host to caves with ancient drawings, one of the biggest tourist attractions. Small houses and large châteaus broke up the countryside.

Something ached in her chest. She wasn't sure if she was missing her family, missing Connor, or some combination of the two.

"Bertrand, do you have a large family?" she asked. It had never really been just the two of them in the car, but now she was eager to find out more about the man who'd been hired to cart them around France.

"Oui, yes, my family all live in Paris. Five generations now."

"Wow. Are you close?" She wondered what it would have been like to grow up knowing your entire family all at once; the people you were related to by blood.

"Yes, Mademoiselle, I believe so. But we have our . . . eh . . . how do you say en anglais . . . *spats*?" He watched her in the mirror.

She nodded.

"But we are blood, family, at the end of the day we come together. Did you have a nice time with yours?"

She smiled absently, her mind elsewhere, "Yes I did, thank you. It was unexpected and wonderful."

It was an amazing thing to be dropped into a brand new family and find that they all liked each other.

Her thoughts turned to other types of families . . . the ones that were created, chosen.

"Are you married, Bertrand?" She instantly regretted asking, she hadn't meant to be nosy, but her straight forward tone and abrupt phrasing had made it sound that way. At least to her.

"Yes, I am. We are still very much in love after twenty-three years." He smiled broadly, clearly proud of the accomplishment and not at all phased by her question.

Something tightened in her chest. She thought of her Irishman and instantly ached for him. Their way forward was unclear. Their radio silence had softened her towards the situation. She'd made her point clear and now she was eager to see how they would weather their first major fight. There was no moving her on her decision; she maintained that he had been paranoid and overprotective, but she had missed him and she hoped that they would be able to get past it.

Bertrand saw the change in her face.

"Monsieur Bannon has been very quiet, not in good humor."

Elizabeth instantly thought something else must have gone wrong at the auction house. "Has anything else happened?" She was alarmed.

Bertrand was aware of all of the security issues. He shook his head, "No, he has been very dark, very sad. That kind of mood . . . a man can only look that way because of a woman."

Her heart lifted, perhaps their time apart had softened him as well. It would certainly make things easier if he admitted he had been wrong. If he learned to ease up so that she didn't wonder whether they would be able to survive each other, as she had during the entire length of their engagement. All four days of it.

Bertrand dropped her off at the apartment at seven. She left her purse by the door and collapsed onto the couch, kicking off her shoes.

Still in Bridgett's white cotton dress she stared up at the ceiling, thinking through everything that had happened in the last few days. It had been a whirlwind. Unexpected, surreal, and so, so much fun. She held onto her family and sent every thought of her fight with Connor away.

She closed her eyes and drifted off to sleep.

Sometime later, she woke to find Connor stroking her legs on the couch.

Rubbing her eyes, she sat up slowly.

"Hi," he said, his voice monotone, devoid of emotion.

His tone irked her. "Hi," she responded in the same flat voice. She hadn't known where they stood, but clearly things were not OK.

He sat back against the couch and crossed his arms. "So any time you want to apologize, I'm ready." He stared straight ahead.

What? *She* apologize?

He didn't need to look at her to know what she was thinking.

"Yes, Lara," his voice started to rise, no longer cool and unaffected. "You kicked me to the curb! One day you're agreeing to marry me, the other, you're throwing me out of your family's château!"

She instantly moved her legs out of his lap, folding them beneath her. A few seconds went by as she tried to breathe in and out, tried to keep herself from flying off the handle. They couldn't both lose it. But the more she thought about it, the more ridiculous the situation seemed.

The more ridiculous it seemed, the more convinced she was that they were going to have it out, *again*.

"You were reckless! Château Fleury isn't exactly a fortress, someone determined enough could have easily gotten in." He was starting to sound like a petulant teenager. "And I deserve an apology."

"Right, because this place," she motioned with her hands at the apartment, "is just like a fortress and there's no way anyone could break in here . . ." she scrunched her eyes together and shook her head.

That particular security breach weighed on him more than any other. If she had been at home when. . . . Connor's eyes bulged, "That's exactly my point!"

His face had turned dark, the way it had looked just before he'd said the words that had set her off before.

The words he'd used twice now: *that's final.*

171

She couldn't hold back anymore, she stood up, even more angry than she had been on Sunday night. "I didn't throw you out! You were being a controlling ass and I thought it would be best if you came back here."

He flailed his arms standing up and meeting her stare, "You threw me out, sent me away, whatever! You were reckless." He ran his fingers through his hair and said something in Gaelic.

"Oh and look what happened?!" she spat. "I'm still here—see, *nothing* happened. What's going on with you? You're devolving into this paranoid controlling asshole!"

"Oh, so it's a crime now to be concerned for your safety? To not want anything to happen to my family?"

"Concern is fine. Control is *not.*" She spoke slowly, deliberately. "I will *never . . .*" she let the word hang in the air, "allow you to control me. No matter what the circumstances. If I feel or think differently, I WILL act according to my own conscience, my own gut. And there will never be anything you can do about it."

He put his hands on his hips. "So that's it?" He shook his head. "You want to be partners in life, but you don't want me to have a say in your life at'all."

"A say?" she turned the word over in her mouth. "When do I tell you what to do or what's best for you? When do I have a say in your life?!"

"Is there something you're not keen on? Something you'd like me to change?" He was defensive.

"This!" She waved her hands signaling whatever was happening to him in that moment.

"Other than that, I've never told you—I never used the words: *that's final.*"

"It's not controlling!" He was defiant. "I'm just trying to keep you secure is all. I don't need to have a say in any other aspect of your life, I just need you to be all right," he repeated again more forcefully, his voice rising.

Why couldn't she see that it was all about keeping her out of harm's way? Keeping her there with him.

"Well unless you want to be like your *father*," she knew she was going into low blow territory before she began, but her anger made it impossible to stop, "then you're just going to have to get over this fear, this thing over my safety. I've accepted the extra security, the bodyguard that follows me around everywhere, but I will never accept you telling me that something is final. I will never accept you saying that something is too dangerous for me to do."

He looked like she had slapped him.

Which, of course, she had.

She knew it was a low blow, but she had to do it. She had to go there and make him see how controlling he was being.

Elizabeth had never met Keanan Grail, and she was glad for it, but she couldn't help but feel that this need to control her movements, to control her life, even out of concern for her safety—came from him.

Originated in the part of him that he always detested; the easiest way to get him to see reason, was to point out the obvious.

She didn't wait to see what affect her words had on him. She put on her sandal wedges quickly and moved around the couch.

"I'm going for a walk," she threw in his general direction, not even bothering to grab her keys.

His voice was harsh, "It's going to rain," he shot at her, still seething.

"So I'll get wet!" she called back over her shoulder before the door slammed behind her.

Just as soon as she stepped outside, it started to sprinkle.

She didn't care. She walked across Rue Vaugirard and took the side gate into the Luxembourg Gardens.

She paced with her hands on her hips in the little area just inside the gate. She was alone, with only a small bench and a tree for company, shielded from the rest of the gardens and the street by a series of tall hedges.

She moved in a circle, taking long deep breaths, trying to steady herself.

She tried to see things from his perspective, tried to see and understand why he would think that it would be all right to hand down edicts, if it concerned her safety.

She could almost see why he would do it, if her life were really in danger. But none of the security issues they had been having had been directed at her, none of them have been violent, there was nothing to suggest that she was in any danger at all.

The raindrops hit the grass and dirt all around her, releasing that smell of sweet ozone, of petrichor. The water evolved from sprinkles, to rain, to a downpour in less than two minutes.

It rained so much harder in the UK and Europe. For all that was made of San Francisco rain, it couldn't compare to the true downpours across the pond.

She continued to pace as the water beat down on her. She opened her arms, letting her head fall back so that the water fell directly on her face.

It was like taking a shower completely clothed, outside, but she didn't care. The physical assault brought her out of her mind and into her senses. There was something truly wonderful about surrendering to the rain, especially in Paris.

"Lara," Connor said from behind her. She whirled around bringing her hands to her hips, the momentary reprieve from her brain hadn't been enough.

She shook her head, and held up a hand to stop him, "No—I'm not ready to deal with you."

"Well you know what?" His voice was hard. "You're just going to have to deal with me. Because you agreed to marry me, or have you changed your mind?"

She tilted her head and flashed him a look that read: *you don't want to go there right now.*

He'd spent the last three days recounting Sunday night, thinking through what she had said—how it had been so easy for her to turn him away.

It was his second greatest fear; that she'd wake up and realize she couldn't deal with his life . . . that it wasn't worth it. Only the thought of her life being in danger trumped it. He'd already had to live through it once; now he wondered if he'd driven her away because he refused to live through it again.

His features suddenly contorted in pain. "Tell me. Have you changed your mind?" The thought had kept him up at night. His brain was screaming at him, telling him not to push her, not to force an answer, but his unpracticed heart needed to know, needed to get it out.

She breathed in through her nose, refusing to take in air through her mouth—if she opened it, she might say something she would regret.

He looked down, his teeth gnashed together. His jaw clenched tight. "I know you called John," he said through gritted teeth.

Elizabeth hadn't noticed up to that point, but her eyebrows were drawn together so fiercely that she'd given herself an actual headache.

His words confused her. She released some of the tension in her forehead involuntarily, instantly feeling some relief.

Huh? Who was John?

She fixed her eyes on him as the rain splashed all around them. "What?" Some of the venom had left her, replaced by bewilderment.

He averted his eyes, focusing them on the hedge to his right that covered most of the black fence. His voice was hard. "He left a message on the machine, at the apartment."

He sounded angry . . . and hurt.

"What?" she said again. "What are you talking about?" She had the strange sense of being truly lost.

"On the machine. There was a message on Monday . . ." he trailed off, some hope made its way into his voice. He moved his eyes from the hedge back to her face. Gaging her reaction.

"*John?* As in the man I dated in San Francisco, *John?*" Her voice went up an octave.

He nodded, eyes narrowed.

"That's ridiculous! Why would I call, *John?*" The idea was laughable. She hadn't given him a second thought. She had an excellent memory and a head for numbers, but she couldn't even recall the three digits that came after the area code of John's number.

Connor watched her closely, seeing the confusion plain on her face. "He left a message saying that he got your email and that he missed you too. . . ."

Elizabeth raised an eyebrow. "I didn't call *anyone* while I was in Méré. And there is no conceivable reason I would ever call or email *John!*"

She thought for a minute. "So is that what's behind this lingering anger? You're mad because I stayed and because you thought I called an ex?"

He didn't say anything, he moved his eyes to the base of the tree behind her. Thinking.

After a minute, he looked up, having tried and failed to work anything out. But his face had changed. The lines in his forehead had smoothed.

He held up his palms, signaling that he had come in peace. Slowly he walked towards her, the rain had soaked his hair and his expensive black blazer.

"You're getting soaked," she observed.

"I don't care." He shook his head.

He stopped when he was two feet in front of her. He shoved his hands in his pockets and looked down at her, sincerity coloring his features.

His voice was like velvet, "How can I make you understand," he started slowly, thinking through each word, "that I would give my life for you?"

His ice blue eyes softened. His perfectly coiffed hair was now disheveled, strands had gotten loose and come forward into his eyes.

Elizabeth watched as the water moved down one of those locks, pooled at the bottom and then dripped down onto the grass below.

His sincerity, his words, went a long way to soften her position. He took another step forward.

"That if something happened to you it would be like–like . . . being shot through the heart. I would want to be the one to die." His dark brows drew together, his eyes watered.

The tension in her face dissolved completely, replaced by something else. He looked like a scared little boy. A scared little boy whose greatest fear . . . was losing her.

He read the thoughts as they crossed her face, taking another step forward until she could feel his breath on her nose.

Her heart stirred, "You can't hide your controlling nature behind your love for me," she whispered into his face. "It isn't OK to lock me away and keep me in a glass box."

"I know, I know," he whispered back, resting his forehead against hers. He stroked her arms bringing her closer an inch at a time.

She stood firm, but let herself be pulled bit by bit, until his lips hovered over hers.

And then all of the anger and frustration she held for him, all of the emotions that she had felt—the good and the bad—over the last several days, mixed with the warm rain pouring down on them. They leaned into each other.

Leaned . . . and then crashed violently.

Their hunger went beyond desire, beyond a need, it was like the world would end if their lips didn't meet.

Hungrily they devoured each other, moving their tongues in concert, exploring each other, until they were completely unhinged.

He tightened his arms around her, crushing her body against his. She could feel his desire, his need for her, through the thin cotton dress.

He pushed her backwards one step. She withdrew, panting, "You can't just—" he stopped her with a kiss. She pulled away again, "You can't ever think that it will be OK to tell me what to do."

"I know, I know," he said between kisses.

"Because if something happens to me as a direct result of a choice *I made*—it was mine to make. You'll never have that right. And you need to be OK with that. Or this isn't going to work," she managed through sheer force of will.

"I'm sorry, I'm sorry," he whispered with his eyes closed, forehead still resting against hers. His words were like a prayer, he was asking for absolution.

She waited for something less vague, closing her eyes to keep from kissing him.

"Jaysus, Mary and Joseph. I love you, Lara. We will find a balance, I promise. I promise to never try to tell you what to do again." He was contrite.

And with that she gave in, kissing him violently under the rain. They were completely soaked as he took another step backwards, and then another, until he pinned her against a tall oak, with a wide base.

Heat had spread to every part of her body, until she didn't know where she was, she didn't know what had happened five minutes ago, she didn't know her own name.

He drove his hips into her, letting his hands venture down to her backside and then down to her leg.

He hitched it up around his hip and pushed his weight into her against the tree.

The bark pricked her through the thin cotton, but she didn't care.

Connor continued his assault diving into her, tasting her lips, and then her neck.

When she thought she was going to pass out from desire, he released her, quickly taking off his jacket and throwing it around her shoulders.

He picked her up and carried her out of the Luxembourg Gardens, across the street, and back up to their apartment.

They crashed through the door. She was straddling him now, Connor had shifted her almost as soon as they'd gotten out of the elevator.

He didn't even bother locking the door to the apartment behind him, just kicked it shut with a bang.

Their reunion was desperate, fierce, almost forceful. He sunk down onto the floor, just past the foyer, laying her down. Quickly, he reached up her legs to throw her panties aside.

She sat up, undoing his belt while he undid his shirt. In record time, they sprung him free, until he was standing in front of her completely naked.

She got one glimpse of his perfect, Adonis-like body, before he came down on her.

Pushing her back onto the floor, he sunk his weight into her body. His lips found her neck, "God, I want you so badly." He sucked on her earlobe.

Their bodies were dripping from the rain. Soaked and slippery, their skin slid together in new ways.

Elizabeth stroked him, until he growled at her ear. She was not gentle.

He reached down between them and dug his fingers into the thin white cotton of her dress. In one move, he flexed his fingers and ripped it open, exposing her heaving breasts and naked sex.

She'd have to get Bridgett another dress, she thought, before taking his face in her hands and bringing him back to her lips, needing to taste him.

Their kisses, were long, deep, almost violent. Their bodies shook with some level of restraint, both not wanting to hurt the other, but finding their need, the culmination of their fight and the strength of their emotions, to be more than either could bear.

"I was miserable without you here," he said against her lips. "Don't ever stay away like that again."

"Don't be an ass," she bit his bottom lip, stilling him, bringing him to attention, "And I won't have to."

His eyes hooded over, he wanted her to feel the extent of his misery, his anger, his despair. He would make her understand what she meant to him, what he would do for her.

His voice was low, just above a growl, "I love you, Lara. I will make you understand." And with that he positioned himself at her entrance, clenched his buttocks and thrust into her with all of his strength.

His muscles tightened as he pounded into her, hard and deep. She screamed out, arching her back as he took her without holding anything back, again and again.

Elizabeth wrapped her legs around him, trying to keep up with his pounding rhythm. He had come unhinged, letting everything he'd been feeling out through his love making. Bringing her into his mind, his body, his soul.

He wanted nothing to separate them, he wanted her to forget where he began and she started, to be fused together. Forever.

Her screams filled the apartment as his assault drove her quickly to that place where time seemed to stop, worlds appeared to collide.

And in the expanse of their apartment, she cried out his name before they both surrendered.

Chapter 12: The Château

"So anyway that's it. I met my, turns out, *great-uncle* Matthieu. Found out that my father was a famous artist. Spent time at my family's château in Méré with my cousins, my aunt, my father, and my great-uncle. Had a fight with Connor ended up staying at the château for three days, came home and made up with Connor."

Elizabeth sat back in her chair and took a sip of her water. She had just finished giving Audre the rundown of her time in Paris over lunch.

"And you already knew about the engagement. Thanks for that, by the way, you could have given me a heads up!" She tilted her head, a look of mock indignation colored her features.

"Why?" Audre said, glass of champagne in hand. "So you could run scared before he had the chance to ask? I love you Babes, but you are too much in your head."

She gave her friend an appraising look, "You're right," Beth allowed. "Besides it was kind of great." She scrunched up her nose like she was embarrassed to admit it.

Audre sat back, her mouth open. "Wow, Liz. You really are making up for lost time. Smushed a whole lot of livin'" she brought her hands together in a ball to indicate *smushed*, "in just a few weeks' time." She sounded like Mel B again.

Beth just shrugged.

Audre shook her head, thinking through all of what her friend had just said.

And then something struck her, "I bet the makeup sex was hot, though?" She speared a piece of broccoli with her fork and popped it into her mouth.

Elizabeth averted her eyes, choosing to find her omelet very interesting indeed.

Audre missed nothing. "Oh! You little minx—I bet it was hot as hell, wasn't it?" Her voice rose, until the couples sitting closest to them stopped talking to look in their direction.

Elizabeth refused to look up.

"Tell me!" Audre protested, tapping her feet beneath the table. "I need some vicarious fun!"

Elizabeth's eyes grew wide as her lips twitched up, "Not. Saying. Another. Word." But then she winked at her friend, and Audre threw her head back, howling.

"No fair. I want a strapping Irishman to sweep me off *my* feet. I want a surprise family to come and take me back to their château," Audre fanned herself with her hand.

Dree was in town on business, looking at a digital collection at the Louvre. She'd worked through the morning, but had lunch and afternoon plans with Beth.

They finished their food all the while catching up on Loryn and her husband, and Wes.

Apparently one of his artists had gotten a bit of international attention and he had been busy making all of the morning show rounds. Making him an even more eligible bachelor in the eyes of the British press.

He'd been well known in the UK for the better part of a decade, but the recent press was turning him into a household name.

They talked about the emails and offers that had come in for Beth. The museum had been contacted by several galleries who were looking for Elizabeth's information.

"Your photo is everywhere, I'll have you know. I think we might use it for our signage—the really big ones. Fungie is going to be huge and you're going to be famous. You'll have your pick of offers. Work for National Geographic, or travel the world and exhibit once every couple of years. The world is your oyster."

Elizabeth didn't know about all of that, but she was lifted by Audre's general elation.

"Happy to know you Elizabeth Lara," Audre held up her glass and cheered to her friend.

And then Beth held up her glass and toasted to Dree for making it happen in the first place.

They finished their food and took the car and Bertrand—at Connor's insistence. Apparently, the kind French driver was packing. Just in case.

She'd met with Brian the day before. He'd given her the keys to her château in Millemont.

She hadn't seen the place yet and thought it would be appropriate to share the experience with her friend.

Audre was bouncing with excitement in her seat. "It's so fashionable," she said.

"What is?"

"You know, to be traveling to the French countryside with one's friends to examine a château left as an inheritance."

Elizabeth raised her eyebrows and laughed as Dree put on her oversized sunglasses, pursed her lips and looked out the window, successfully playing the celebrity.

She settled into her seat and thought about what Brian had told her.

According to him, her inheritance was an eighteenth century, five-bedroom house with three master suites and two regular bedrooms. It had a library, formal dining room, kitchen, and who knows what else.

He assured her that it had been recently updated, although recently was a subjective term in France; it could mean three years or thirty. Brian didn't know when they had been done, if they had been done at Mags' instruction, or if she had purchased the property already finished.

Fifty minutes later, the black town car approached the house.

There was an actual wrought iron gate that led to a long paved driveway; her inheritance stood at the end of the path. Elizabeth handed the code to Bertrand as her eyes fell on a black sign with beautiful gold letters.

The sign on the gate read, "Château Plaisir."

They pulled up in front of the house. A structure with two doors set off center and slightly raised from the rest of the façade, with three sets of windows over two stories. The pitched roof flattened into a plateau, in the traditional French style.

"Wow," she and Audre said together.

Elizabeth was stunned. Her feet propelled her forward automatically, up the short steps, spaced several feet apart, past the manicured greenery, and up to the black doors that popped against the ivory façade and blue-gray roof.

Her fingers traced a design carved into the right door: two small hearts interlocked together and tilted on an angle so that they looked like a single butterfly. She knew without a doubt that Mags had placed it there.

She turned the key in the lock and stepped inside.

The front room was a massive great hall, framed on the second floor by an intricate black railing that ran between several columns and the second story windows. It was so large she wondered how there could actually be any space left for the other rooms in the house.

The Château was beautiful from the driveway, but it didn't look all that big. From outside she estimated that it was a third of the size of Château Fleury. But this grand space, whatever it was, was a very generous size.

Light flooded in from ten massive windows stacked in columns of five.

Beth's eyes were wide, her eyebrows raised—they'd been frozen in place since she'd walked in. "Maybe it will look smaller with furniture?" she said to herself.

Audre came in behind her, quickly appraising the situation.

"Veerry nice," she mused walking around the space with efficiency and moving on to the next room.

Elizabeth walked to the center and looked up, turning slowly to take it all in.

Mags had bought this place a few years ago? Why hadn't she moved here? It would have been a lovely place for her . . . in the end.

And then a thought struck her, and in that moment she knew. She knew why her great-aunt had chosen to stay in Berkeley. She'd stayed because of Elizabeth.

She'd managed to cut herself off from everything and everyone, except her work. Mags was her one lifeline to the outside world. And she knew it.

She bit the inside of her lip to keep herself from crying. Drawing her arms into her chest, she clutched her heart. It ached for Mags. It ached for Matthieu.

It ached for their love story.

It spanned fifty years, but how she would have written a different ending for them.

"Babes! These masters are enormous! Come up."

She dabbed at her eyes, wishing with all her heart that it had been different for Mags. The feelings of guilt were kept at bay by her great-aunt's video to Matthieu . . . it had all happened the way it was supposed to. If only life had been kinder.

It had been some time since Beth had thought about an afterlife. About what came in next, *if* anything came next. She'd certainly felt Mags' spirit throughout her journey and felt her hand in nearly everything, but now Beth needed there to be something beyond this life, so that Mags and Matthieu could finally be together . . . somewhere.

Elizabeth followed the sound of Audre's voice, climbing the stairs to her left.

Each master had at least two walls of windows and a massive chandelier in the middle. The château was unfurnished, but move-in ready.

Audre wandered from room to room, even more excited than Beth. She kept talking to herself about what would be perfect for this space or that space. How a mirror would reflect the light *just so* and create a dramatic feature.

Listening to Audre talk about her creative plans was almost as fun as discovering every room.

"Gosh, you could have lovely parties here," she said dreamily.

Then she turned to Elizabeth, "Do you know what you want to do with the space yet, Luv? You're going to keep it, of course. Maybe use it as a vacation estate?"

191

"You mean have I decided what I'm going to do with this big ass house? How I'm going to fill it with *stuff?*" The château was so magnificent, it had reduced her vocabulary to that of a ten-year-old boy.

Her eyebrows shot up, "In the five minutes I've been here?" She was overwhelmed. "I like to look through a lens Dree, my creativity doesn't extend to instantly creating an interior design plan for the biggest space I've ever owned in my life."

"All right, all right. No need to get testy." Audre pursed her lips and continued going through each room.

"If you like, I can throw some ideas together for you," Audre's eyes were bright with inspiration. She was clearly waiting for Beth to ask her for help.

"Are you really that in need of vicarious fun? Don't they run you ragged at that museum of yours?"

Her face fell, "Yes, they do. But sometimes I feel a strong need to flex my creative muscle, you know? After a while . . . the paperwork, dealing with artists and all of the legal issues that come with digital rights—it gets to me, Liz. So . . . *sometimes* I like to take on projects that are more creative, more fun, but still firmly rooted in art and design."

"Are you offering to be my interior designer?"

"Depends," she hesitated, narrowing her eyes, "are you *offering* me the job of interior designer?"

"Sure," Elizabeth shrugged, more than happy to hand over the project, "but under one condition."

"What's that, Luv?"

"That you let me pay you *extremely* well!"

Audre threw her head back, "You will not pay me a DIME." She raised an eyebrow and dared Beth to argue with her.

Elizabeth put her hands on her hips, taking a power stance. "Oh yes I will pay you. I refuse to take advantage of our friendship."

"Please," Audre rolled her eyes and waved a hand at her. "You'd be doing me the favor, taking on a place like this? If I ever wanted to branch out into interior design, this," she motioned wildly with her hands, "would be the crown jewel of my portfolio."

"I still insist on paying you." Beth crossed her arms.

Audre laughed again, this time louder as she walked out of the third master. "We'll see about that." And then she stopped at the door and turned back, "You can pay me in margaritas," she smiled. "How's that?"

After thoroughly inspecting the château, they took a peak at the massive lawn that spanned out from the house and eventually sloped upwards to a grove of trees and a more wild looking forest some distance away. A large hill appeared to border the wilderness, shielding the house and manicured gardens from the world. They didn't make it very far before Elizabeth's phone started ringing.

She'd set her ringtone to be a song that Kilian had recently sent her. It was just his voice with an acoustic guitar. The song was folksy with hints of R&B, a cross between Ed

Sheeran and The Lumineers, with the bonus of his endearing Irish accent. She'd sent him notes on the previous version and after some back and forth they'd gotten the song to a place they both loved.

"Ohhh, what's that?" Audre asked as Beth hit the "answer" button.

"It's a song a friend wrote, it's called *The Guide to Midnight*, isn't it great?"

Audre scrunched up her nose. "It's lovely, and he sounds delicious. I bet he's gorgeous. He is, isn't he?"

Beth opened her mouth to answer, but held up a finger instead, putting the phone to her ear. "Hello?"

"Lara, promise me you'll keep Bertrand close." His voice was heightened, alarmed.

"Well hello to you, too." She tried to keep things light.

"Sorry, Luv. Hi. I trust your visit with Audre and the house is all you hoped?"

She smiled into the phone. "It'll do."

"I'm glad, I'm glad," he said absently.

She could tell he was trying to be pleasant instead of alarmist.

Elizabeth sighed. "What's wrong?"

"Er . . . just please keep Bertrand close, all right?"

"What's wrong?" she repeated, taking a few steps away from Audre.

"The PI I had looking for Stephen has found that he has family in France, just a few hours away. I don't actually know if he's in the country, it's just made me jumpy. Please, for me, stay close to Bertrand?" He was careful to keep the request firmly in the realm of *request*.

"OK, sure. But Connor, don't worry so much. Honestly, he probably hasn't even fully healed from the last time he saw me—I doubt very much he'd be in a hurry to do it again. Just relax." She tried to soothe him through the phone.

"All right, Luv. I know you can take care of yourself . . . just keep your eyes open. I love you."

And with that they said their goodbyes, making plans for a romantic night in.

Elizabeth turned back to Audre who was busy searching for something on her phone.

"What's the name of the chap who wrote that song?" She didn't look up.

"Kilian. He's the one I was with when I took that picture of Fungie and the great white."

"I can't find that song anywhere."

Elizabeth took her friend by the arm and led her back towards the house, "That's because he's an emerging artist. He hasn't been signed yet."

"Really?" Audre's eyes glittered with some new thought.

They walked back to the car and drove to Méré; Elizabeth was eager to introduce her friend to her new family.

They found only Matthieu and Alexandre at home.

Audre fawned over Beth's father. She knew him by name, but had never met him. She got along with Matthieu as well, all three of them sharing a background in art.

Elizabeth stepped back and watched as her friend charmed the two older men. By the time she was through, she may or may not have gotten Alexandre to come to London to give a small exhibition at her museum. And Matthieu may or may not have agreed to give a lecture at the museum at some as yet undetermined date.

Elizabeth looked on happily as her worlds collided. Her old friend and her new family, meeting in some beautifully curated world of art.

CHAPTER 13: SURPRISE!

After a week, Connor and Elizabeth settled into an easy routine.

She continued to go out and walk the streets of Paris, finding new subjects to photograph, and slowly forming an idea of what she might do with all of the offers that had started to pile up—all while adjusting to the idea that a member of the security team was always nearby. After a couple of days, she'd started to forget they were there.

Connor was spending less time at the auction house. There hadn't been any new security issues to deal with, and so he had taken a backseat and delegated the remaining work to his very capable team.

He had already sold a handful of items at a small private auction he had held for twenty of his best collectors.

They were his top clients and had received the space and the new additions well. That was half the battle he had told Beth, winning over the people who made the majority of the big purchases.

The pieces he chose to go after were always off the beaten track type items. Objects that might be historically interesting, but did not have the same value as a Monet.

Still, they were highly valuable and highly sought after by a select group of people who had very specific, very discerning tastes and were highly competitive with each other. It was a built in market.

He spent more time at the apartment, the majority of his work-related duties now relegated to identifying new pieces, both known and unknown, to go out into the world and find. To add to his collections.

Elizabeth called it his *treasure-mapping* phase. She was just glad to see him more often.

And so they settled into an easy routine of domesticity, content in their own separate endeavors. Always happy to come together at the end of the day—with a few afternoon trysts thrown in for good measure.

There had only been one single blip, a small ripple in an otherwise calm lake. The tabloids had decided to shine the spotlight back on them.

The headline read: *Committed! Irish Noble Taken!* with a shot of them kissing and holding hands outside of Le Meurice.

Elizabeth was happy to note that the rags affected her far less than they would have just a few weeks before. It was getting easier. It had only been a week of easier, but it was a relief to know that it could get more manageable just the same.

On Saturday, they returned for another family dinner at Château Fleury.

They spent the fifty minute ride from Paris, tightly wrapped in each other's arms, neither wanting to let go of the other.

Since their reunion on the floor of the apartment the week before, their physical connection had become paramount. They'd become more or less inseparable whenever they were in the same room together.

They talked and laughed and kissed, enjoying their blissful reprieve from all things heavy and dramatic. It was a relief to remember that, when left undisturbed, they were an easy couple; a good, natural fit.

Bertrand drove up the curved driveway, to the massive house. Unlike Château Plaisir, the façade of Fleury was all on one plane. One massive plane with seven columns of windows stacked on top of each other. Its pitched roof resulted in a much larger plateau in the typical French style.

Usually, the pathway was flooded with light from the massive windows, but as they got out of the car, the house looked abandoned. All of the lights were off.

She checked her phone. It was eight—they were perfectly on time.

"Are you sure it was today?" Connor asked now by her side.

"Yes, *Saturday*," she said with a good dose of sarcasm, "it's not like I have so many dinner dates with my family that I can't keep track."

He laughed and took her hand, ringing the doorbell.

They waited.

When no one came to the door she tried looking through the windows, but all of the long drapes appeared to be drawn.

"That's strange, they never close these. Let's try around back." Elizabeth led the way as she went around the massive château along the side wall and through the small gate that led to the backyard.

When they reached the large concrete covered patio, they were suddenly blinded by a show of bright lights and at least thirty people yelling, "*Surprise!*"

Elizabeth squinted and tried to smile through the pain the sudden light had inspired. Blinking wildly until her eyes acclimated to her surroundings, she found some familiar face.

Audre was there between Matthieu, Alexandre, and Brian. She stepped forward and greeted them, "Welcome Babes to your engagement party!" she gestured to the crowd as they cheered.

Beth leaned in to kiss Audre on both cheeks, "Dree what are you doing here, what is this?" She'd expected a quiet dinner and now felt self-conscious in her flowy peasant tank top, skinny jeans and boots.

"Well I got on so well with your new family that I wondered what they thought about my throwing you an engagement party. They offered to host and so it just came together in the last week! Loryn is here with her husband. They took the Eurostar with me."

Elizabeth glanced in the direction that Audre was pointing. Her beautiful blonde friend was wearing a short blue dress with perfectly straight hair. She was holding hands with her Ken doll look-alike husband. Elizabeth waved at them, hoping they'd get a chance to talk.

Audre took her by the hand, separating her from Connor. A second later she was enveloped by a sea of women all coming forward to kiss her on both cheeks. She looked back at Connor who had been taken to a corner and offered some type of amber spirit in a glass.

The next hour was spent moving amongst her guests. Being introduced again and again to different people, friends of her cousins, friends of her aunt, people from the village.

Although she'd met some of them in her exploration of Méré with Renée and Bridgett, many were new faces. All of them seemed to be very happy to be there.

Renée had explained that she had become quite the talk of the town. A favorite topic of gossip, but that everyone who had met her had said nice things about Alexandre's lost American love child. Who, apparently, was a famous photographer in her own right.

Elizabeth laughed.

At some point, more people had begun to file in until the massive lawn and patio were nearly filled.

Audre found her, shaking her head, "Where did all of these people come from? I don't understand. It was supposed to be an intimate party of thirty or forty, but more people just keep showing up! They all seem to be bringing food and refreshments—so at least there's that, but who is this lot?"

Renée sidled up to the pair of them, "This would be the entire village," she smiled. "It happens this way, sometimes. If you have a party and they find out, they'll all just show up, always with something to offer as is only polite."

Renée surveyed the crowd, finding her sister flirting with one of the handsome servers holding a tray of champagne flutes.

"Plus," she continued, "Bridgett took a photo and mentioned you and Connor. She posted it on all of her accounts. I'm sure it was picked up somewhere along the way and this," she motioned with her hand, "is the result."

She squeezed Beth shoulder. "Welcome to the family," she smiled through her teeth. Her eyes read, *welcome to the crazy*. She took a sip of champagne before walking off to find her partner Nicolle.

Audre stared daggers at the back of Bridgett's shoulder length black hair. "The French!" she threw up her hands in exasperation, saying it just above her normal speaking voice—and being rewarded with several severe looks.

She quickly clasped her hands and recovered, ". . .Are *lovely* people!" she gave the crowd a strained smile, nodding at everyone who had started to give her scathing looks. Some of them muttered obscenities under their breath.

She took the champagne flute out of Elizabeth's hand and downed it, "Christ I have no idea where all of these people came from, but apparently welcome to your village, Elizabeth Lara!"

"Breathe Dree."

She brought her shoulders up to her ears and dropped them quickly, attempting to breathe. "Sorry your engagement party is such a mess, Babes."

Elizabeth leaned in to give her friend a big hug. "Are you kidding? This is amazing." She took her hand, "Thank you."

And then Beth remembered something else she'd meant to speak to Audre about.

"In fact, I was thinking the other day . . ."

"You *were*. What about?" Audre was only half listening, still staring worriedly at the crowd.

"Well in addition to being my interior designer, I thought maybe you could also be my maid of honor."

Audre turned to look at her.

Beth smiled expectantly.

Audre narrowed her eyes, "Really?"

Beth nodded.

"Really?" Audre said again more excited. "Yes, of course!" She hugged Beth fiercely and then launched into question after question about what Beth was planning, and when she wanted to do it, and several more questions she didn't have the answers to.

"It won't be for a while. We've got plenty of time to think about all of that." Beth's eyes grew wide, she waved her hands, shooing all of Audre's questions away.

"Well what are we talking about here? Six months . . . a year?" Dree asked.

Beth considered, "A year . . . *maybe* two?" She shrugged.

Audre gave her a *what?!* with her eyes.

Before her friend could pepper her with any more questions, she took evasive action, "Well since I'm out," Elizabeth looked pointedly at the empty champagne flute now in Audre's hand. "I'm going to the loo and then I'm going to find a replacement drink."

She looked around for servers with champagne trays, but didn't see anyone.

"Well good luck!" Audre said throwing up her hands. "I certainly hope there's alcohol left."

Elizabeth walked into the château past the dining room area and into the kitchen.

Everyone appeared to be outside except for the serving staff who were busy opening more bottles of champagne, and putting more flutes on trays before heading back outside.

She decided to keep walking through the kitchen, into the grand hall and back out the front door. Some of the lights were on inside the house now, but they were at the back, leaving the front of the house wonderfully dark, with very little light pollution.

Elizabeth crossed her arms over her white top and looked up into the sky. Breathing in the warm night air as a breeze picked up wafting honeysuckle and jasmine into her face, she let her head fall back.

She remembered what Mags had always told her about the stars, *that they were our constant reminder of how small and big life could be, how infinite and ephemeral.*

What a life she had managed to create, in spite of the decade-long detour she'd taken. Perhaps everything did happen for a reason, like Mags had always said.

If she had made different choices, maybe they would have led her to stand under a different sky on that night. And what a glorious night it was. She was glad to be standing under those very stars, in that very corner of the world.

She closed her eyes, giving thanks to whatever God or Universe was responsible for bringing such wonderful people into her life.

She gave thanks because she had been saved from a life unlived, from a life that was never meant for her.

She heard the door open behind her. A soft female voice came to her side, "Would you like a drink Mademoiselle?" She held out a tray, there was only one champagne flute left.

Elizabeth smiled at the woman with short black hair, "Yes, thank you." She took the flute as the woman disappeared back into the château.

She sipped her champagne happily, grateful she had a chance to catch her breath, to be alone with her thoughts. Grateful for all the events that had brought her to that moment.

She looked back up at the stars, thinking they looked like diamonds against the pitch black.

Then suddenly, her ears rung with the sound of breaking glass, as the diamonds turned into shooting stars and the world turned upside down.

Beth opened her eyes to the cold, damp, darkness.

Her vision was blurred.

Instinctively she brought a hand to her head.

She blinked trying to focus.

Her other hand felt the ground. Her fingernails dug into the cold, damp, dirt.

Her eyes couldn't focus on anything and then she realized why.

There wasn't enough light. The only light was coming from behind her. It was just enough to make out the hole of the cave.

She tried to remember how she'd gotten there, but she heard the footsteps approach. She resumed her position on the ground, not wanting her kidnapper to know she'd regained consciousness.

A flashlight shone in her face.

Don't squint Beth, don't move a muscle.

The light passed over her body and then she heard the footsteps retreat.

She looked up to see the person disappearing just beyond the hole.

The cave was musty. It smelled of old earth.

Beth sat up, tuning into her senses.

She could hear water dripping from somewhere nearby. And something else moving. Bats maybe?

She focused on her sense of hearing, trying to push out beyond the cave.

There was nothing. No road. No cars. No people.

She wasn't in one of the well-known series of caves often frequented by the tourists.

Think Beth. Think!

How had this happened? How long had she been gone?

She was just in bed with Connor that morning. Or was it yesterday? *Shit!* She had no sense of how much time she'd lost.

Wasn't there a party? She remembered being at Château Fleury.

Her stomach growled, but she didn't need to go to the bathroom. What did that mean?

When was her last meal?

Her head started pounding, or rather she reconnected with her pounding head. She used her fingers to check her skull for bumps and gashes.

There was nothing.

She'd been drugged then? She remembered looking up at the stars and then it all went blank. It had to have been the champagne—and it had to have been something very strong to knock her out so quickly.

Connor, Matthieu, and Brian must have people out looking for her by now.

The whole village maybe.

What did these people . . . or person want?

The questions flooded her brain, causing the pain to shoot through her temples like a needle. She pressed both palms to her head and squeezed, making a vice.

She went through her pockets, checking for her phone. Taking stock of everything she had on her.

There was nothing. They must have taken it all. Whoever *they* were.

She had nothing on her except the clothes on her back, her shoes . . . and the ring on her finger.

Chapter 14: Long Ago

Elizabeth shifted her weight, getting to her hands and knees. Even in this position she teetered back and forth, almost toppling back to the ground.

She took a deep breath and tried to steady herself.

Focusing like she was a tight rope walker, she positioned one foot underneath her and then the other, clenching all of her muscles to stand upright.

She walked forward, towards the light, being certain to stay close to the rough cave walls. The protrusions and jagged edges scraped her bare arms as she put one foot in front of the other, not quite in control of her limbs.

As she approached the entrance to the cave, she heard voices. Quickly, she flattened herself against the wall and listened. There was only one voice.

A female voice.

Beth edged herself towards the hole where sunlight spilled through. She angled her head, trying to see what was beyond the cave.

She snapped her head back towards the darkness, as the light stung her to complete blindness. She tried again, first focusing on the light spilling through onto the dirt in front of her then the jagged cave walls, and then she followed the light, breathing into the pain as her eyes attempted to adjust to the brightness.

She welcomed the new pain, it lessened the pounding in her head.

A picture finally formed through the light. There was a woman with short black hair. *Spiky* black hair. She had fair skin and a slender frame. The server who'd offered her the champagne.

She was taller than Beth and pacing back and forth in front of the entrance. There didn't appear to be anyone with her. In one hand she carried a gun, in the other a knife.

There was something familiar about her, something that went beyond the brief encounter at the party. Elizabeth quickly searched her memory, where had she seen her before?

She tried to think back, but the blood surged through her brain, pulsing, throbbing.

And then she remembered, a pair of dark eyes in a fair face, the same spiky black hair. It was longer now, but unmistakably the same.

Elizabeth had been walking up the steps of a small stage in Dingle. Just having been asked to judge the dessert contest at the Food & Drink Festival.

She had caught sight of the woman as she ascended the stage. Beth remembered wondering who she was looking at with such unmasked loathing. Now, the truth was plain. At that point, Elizabeth had done nothing to cause offense to anyone . . . except being seen in public with Connor.

It was always about him, she put some of the pieces together.

There was something else as well, a picture. A picture on Facebook, a group of people at Cambridge. . . .

She was an ex-girlfriend, or someone he'd slept with. One of the poor souls who had wanted more than he could give.

Quickly, she assessed the situation, trying to decide on a course of action. How could she use her powers of manipulation to find a way through to the other side?

Just then, the woman stopped pacing and headed back for the cave.

Elizabeth's reflexes were too slow, she didn't have time to get back to her position on the ground and play unconscious again.

So she flattened herself against the wall and waited. When the woman took her first step into the cave Elizabeth took her shot. In one clumsy movement, Elizabeth launched herself at the woman trying to knock the weapons away.

But the remnants of the drug in her system, made her too weak to be effective. The spiky haired woman dodged the attack easily and Beth fell to her knees at the mouth of the cave. She heard someone curse and then darkness.

Elizabeth opened her eyes, the world had gone from dark, to blurry. She winced as her head screamed at her. The throbbing had gone from bearable, to sending her to the edges of unconsciousness.

She looked down at her hands, they were tied with jagged rope that bit into her skin. She tried to move her legs and then realized that they were tied at the ankles as well.

"Don't bother," the woman said.

She could hear it now, the Irish accent underneath.

Her abductor sat with her legs straight in front of her, her back against the wall of the cave, next to the opening, opposite Beth.

A gun in her hand, a knife at her side. She held the gun casually in her lap, but it was firmly trained on Beth.

"You ruined everything," she said with pure hatred in her voice. "It wasn't supposed to be like this. He was supposed to finally see that *we* belong together."

At least she was talking. Whoever this woman was, she was clearly fixated on Connor. If she could just get her to keep talking. . . .

"Who are you?" Beth said gently, trying to focus on her voice, to sound welcoming, calm.

"I'm Alyson," she said it like Beth should know her name, "Connor and I are involved. Meant to be, really. But then you came along and it all went to shite."

Something in her stomach dropped, what did she mean *involved?*

"I'm sorry if he hurt you. I didn't know." She kept things vague, giving Alyson the opportunity to explain further.

"He didn't hurt me," Alyson shook her head like the idea was a ridiculous one; she was on the verge of saying more.

Elizabeth encouraged her, "No, he definitely hurt you. Or you wouldn't be here with me now."

"He didn't *hurt* me." Her voice rose, she leaned forward.

It was a risk to continue down this line of questioning, to get a rise out of her. She was clearly unstable, but her gut told her that she needed to keep Alyson talking.

"What did he do? Did he sleep with you and then forget about you?"

Alyson moved the gun from her lap to the ground next to her, her finger still on the trigger.

She leaned forward, "No! He wouldn't do that. We're waiting." Her face changed, her voice calmed with the last sentence. Like the idea of waiting to be with him was something she held onto, something that kept her going.

That was it, that was her shot.

Elizabeth changed her voice again, taking on that of a girlfriend wanting to hear about her friend's new boyfriend, "How did you two meet?"

Alyson's eyes narrowed and then something in them went unfocused, they drifted up above Beth's head, "We grew up together," she said dreamily.

"In Dingle. He was three years ahead of me but I always knew we had a connection. And then I went to Cambridge and we dated," she nodded matter-of-factly.

"Oh?" Her stomach turned, but she kept her voice in girlfriend zone. "How long did you two date? What was your first kiss?" She followed up with the second question quickly to keep her occupied, fixated on the fantasy of Connor.

"Oh it was just once," Alyson let her head fall further backwards against the cave wall. "There was a group of us from the same area in Ireland. We made plans to go out, but everyone bailed at the last minute and so it was just the two of us."

Her shoulders rose to her ears, she let go of the gun on the ground and clasped her hands together in front of her. She smiled at the memory, lost in some other world, that wasn't this one.

"So what did you do? It must have been romantic," Beth prodded.

"Oh it was! We went into a pub and talked about Dingle, and growing up with all the quirks of the village, we talked about Fungie and the things he missed from home. And then at the end of the night . . ." her voice trailed off.

She brought one hand up to her lips, "We almost kissed. I knew then," her eyes refocused on Beth's face, "that it was only a matter of time. We were meant to be."

Beth smiled, using all of her skills of manipulation.

"I mean, I watched him with all of those women throughout the years. But I knew it was nothing serious, he would scarcely spend a week with them." She laughed, it was a mocking laugh. A *they were all so stupid*, type of laugh.

All at once, Alyson seems to wake from her dream, the sheer hatred reentered her eyes as she trained them on Beth.

"And then you came along. I was home in Dingle visiting my father, when I saw you two together at the festival," she spat.

"I could tell it was different. *He* was different, he kept smiling and laughing and looking for little reasons to touch you. And then he went and made you a judge. You were just so smug walking up the steps, everyone could see that he favored you in a way that he'd never done with anyone.

"He'd never gone 'round with anyone locally—he'd never even gone to an event in the village with a woman. He singled you out and everyone knew it.

"But I knew that you were just some clueless American. I took those pictures at the town hall and sent them out to the papers. I thought maybe it would scare you off, to see how big his life really was.

"He seemed to be doing a pretty good job of making you think that he was just this simple Irish guy, with cool blue eyes and a lot of money. But I knew, I knew it would reach you.

"And then he left for Africa and you went to England. I thought, it was finally over. I thought he'd finally seen reason. How much could he care for you if he could just leave like that? And not take you with him?

"You clearly weren't together while he was away. Those pictures of him and Sade, proved that. I thought it was finally my turn. So I followed him to London. But then I saw

215

him renew his overtures to you. You were this little *bitch* I couldn't get rid of."

If looks could kill, Elizabeth would already be dead. But still she focused on every little detail she presented to Alyson. Every blink, every nod, she even focused on radiating a friendly energy, shoving all of her real thoughts so far down, she could almost believe the lie she was presenting herself.

"So I found my way into his hotel room, papa was a locksmith you see—I paid attention—and electronic keys . . . well it doesn't take a genius," she said as an aside, "hoping to find *something*. Pictures of other women, conversations anything that I could use to make you end things. Anything that would make you choose Cartwright. But there was nothing."

Then Alyson's voice turned to that of a cold sociopath, and Beth wondered for the first time whether she would make it out of the cave alive. "So I hired a man to drug you."

At that Elizabeth's blood curdled, Connor had been right. She had been targeted, the incident with Jeff was no coincidence.

"I had him follow you and everything seemed to be working according to plan, he gave you *twice* the normal dosage. I watched from across the street." She laughed hard, full of acid.

"But then you walked right out of that pub, on your own two feet. And then Connor himself comes to your rescue." She laughs again, harder. "And then Cartwright!"

She gave Beth a cold stare, "You *are* popular with the boys. You must have a magic gooter." Her eyes grew wide.

"What is it with you? Is it the cool California girl attitude? Are you crazy in bed? Is that what he likes? Do you interrogate him?"

Elizabeth felt the muscles in her jaw tighten, but remained focused. She held on to her girlfriend zone voice like her life depended on it, "You must love him very much," she said lightly, sweetly.

Some of the sting drained from Alyson's face. "Yes, I do. You have no business being with him, you don't know what his life entails."

"I can tell that you care for him very deeply. You should try calling him, talking to him, so you two can finally be together."

It was killing her to talk this way, but she knew she had to try.

"I did call several times. I called Bannon's again and again . . . everyone but him answered."

Another piece of the puzzle fell into place.

"That must have made you angry," she continued.

Maybe if she could keep the girlfriend thing going and get on her good side, she could make Alyson think that it was Connor who she really hated.

Although if successful, that plan came with a whole different set of difficulties. Alyson might kill her to get back at him.

"It did." Her eyes grew bright, Beth let understanding color her face, empathy.

"Yeah one time I was just outside and no one answered, it was so frustrating! Sometimes I think he does it on purpose—to test me."

"You should have done something, something to get his attention."

"I did." She sat forward another degree, "One time I got so mad that I threw a rock through the window."

"Did you come by his apartment at all?"

"Yes, I watched you two leave together," all the vitriol was back.

Shit.

"I'd been trying to do something else, to drive a wedge between the two of you. So I let myself in and found the phone he had installed. I sent an email pretending to be you to that man you used to date in San Francisco, *John.* I told him how much you missed him and left the phone number.

"I wasn't sure he'd called, but then I noticed that you hadn't been to the apartment in days. And then I thought, I'd finally done it," she smiled briefly.

Beth tried to picture it all. How had this woman managed to evade the entire security team? She'd been watching the apartment so closely—how was that possible?

"But then those nasty photographs came out in the papers." She snorted, disbelieving, "He proposed to you!" She was disgusted.

"To you! And that's when I knew I had to do something bigger."

Beth's head throbbed just them, it was the most pain she'd ever been in her life. She cringed, trying to breathe normally. The sudden agony derailed her girlfriend zone strategy, "So why take me? Where do you see this going?"

She bit the inside of her lip just as soon as the words escaped her mouth. She hoped she hadn't blown it.

Alyson let her head fall back against the wall, she expelled all the air from her lungs, "It wasn't supposed to be like this, I was supposed to be able to take you far away. I rented a little house out in the middle of nowhere.

"I was going to make it look like you were just too overwhelmed, too incapable of dealing with his life and had just left him. I had it all figured out, but then the police blocked the roads and I was forced to find somewhere to else to go."

"And now?" Beth winced again.

"And now," she put her hands to her head, "I don't know."

Then Alyson's eyes blazed suddenly, "SHUT UP! Just *SHUT UP!*" She rocked back and forth, hugging herself. "This is all going to work out. Connor will see how much I love him, see what I'm willing to do for him, and he'll choose me. He'll see it in my eyes, just like I knew."

Beth thought about what to say next. "You know, I *was* feeling overwhelmed." She tried to make herself sound vulnerable, let this woman into her confidence. "I didn't know about the engagement party. I was planning on letting him down easy after the dinner I thought I was having with my family."

Alyson looked at her again, a measure of hope touched her eyes. "Really?"

Beth nodded, trying her best to sell it. "Yeah, it's too much. The tabloids, the security. Do you know that I've had a bodyguard following me around for weeks now?"

"Yeah, I noticed him."

"I like to be free, I like to wander. It's just too much."

Alyson nodded, "It can be a bit much when you don't know what to expect."

It was working.

"Yeah, and I had just lost my great-aunt Magdalen— she raised me. So you know it was just kind of comforting to be with him. I thought I could be different, I thought I could be happy settling down. But that life is not for me."

Alyson stayed quiet, pensive.

"Have you ever lost anyone Alyson?"

She nodded, her eyes watered. "My father, two months ago."

"I'm so sorry. Sometimes, when you're dealing with grief, you just need different types of people in your life, you know? I think maybe that's what Connor was for me. He was so different from every other guy I had ever dated. It was unpredictable and exciting for a while. But I like to be in control, I like to have a plan. And Connor is sweet, but he isn't for me."

Alyson stilled. "So . . . you were really going to leave him?"

Beth nodded, slowly, like it pained her to admit it.

It was working.

"You know," she tried to tread lightly, "if you let me go then I can do what I planned on doing. And then he would be free and you could talk."

Alyson's eyes went from holding some level of understanding to letting in an equal amount of suspicion. She narrowed her eyes considering.

"No." She stood up taking the gun with her, "I think, for now I'll keep you here."

But her voice didn't hold the same level of vitriol that it did before.

Elizabeth's heart lightened, a few more conversations and maybe, *just* maybe.

Alyson walked over to Beth and gagged her, "I have to go check on something. I don't know this area, but I can't have you calling out for help just in case."

And with that she walked out of the cave, disappearing into the light.

Beth's eyes drooped, exhausted from the exertion of concocting a story and trying to sound like a friend to this woman who had made it her life's mission to ruin hers.

She needed to sleep, to rest. But she didn't think she should close her eyes, she needed to stay awake, stay alert.

But it wasn't up to her. She'd expended an extraordinary amount of energy controlling every micro expression, every movement.

Her vision blurred and then she was gone again.

CHAPTER 15: DANCING ON CLIFFS

She woke to find someone pushing her upright. She was still on the floor, her legs extended and tied in front of her.

She looked up into the face of the person jostling her.

It was familiar, but not welcome.

His hair was cut, his face smooth, his eyes no longer glassy and unfocused, like they had been the night he had held her at gunpoint.

It was Stephen.

He removed her gag.

"You? You're part of this." Beth looked up into his face.

It wasn't a question.

She kicked herself mentally, now angry that she hadn't taken Connor's concerns about him more seriously.

He'd been right all along, he was behind it. They were probably working together. And now, it would cost her everything.

"No, no," he held up his hands. He started to untie her legs, "No, I came to the party last night. I saw you taken.

Saw that woman, Alyson, put you into a car." His voice was filled with anxiety, his Irish accent thick.

"I ran up behind it, but I was too late. I didn't know if I should get back in my car and follow or go into the party to find Bannon." He was having problems with the small knots at her legs.

"I found him and told him what happened. He almost knocked the shit out of me, I didn't have time to explain why I had come. Didn't get to tell him that I was there to apologize. I told him about the car and what I had seen—I don't know what happened after that.

"But I got in my car and went in the direction that she had taken you. The police blocked off the roads, so I started turning down dirt pathways or anywhere that a car might be able to drive.

"I saw her car hidden behind some shrubs next to this hole. I called Bannon and told him where I was, but the connection is terrible out here. I don't know how much got through—hopefully someone is on their way. I waited for her to leave and then I came in. We have to hurry."

"You came to help me? But why would you bother?" Between the drugs and the blow to the back of the head, Elizabeth was incapable of logically considering whether she should be trying to talk the man trying to help her out of untying her legs.

"Because I owed you," he winced, trying to undo the knots.

"I threw a knife into your wrist." She looked at his arm. It was still bandaged. She realized the reason it was taking him so long to untie her was that he had lingering weakness in his right hand. He couldn't close all of his fingers.

"Yes, but I know you could've had my arse thrown away. You could have ruined my life, but you chose not to. I know that.

"If it were my old man," he laughed hard. "He would've locked me up and thrown away the key."

He breathed into the pain as he continued to fumble with the cords at her feet.

"In the hospital, they got me clean and really helped me. I was on some pretty heavy shit when I came at you."

He shook his head, some level of self-loathing touched his features.

"I went to stay with my uncle and my cousin about an hour from here. They were always nice to me. Knew how I'd grown up, with my 'da. So they took me in.

"I heard you were in France and that you were having a party tonight in Méré. I didn't think, I just borrowed my cousin's car. Ya see, I've felt like a complete shit for what I did. And rightly so.

"I didn't know what I was going to do exactly, probably just come up to you and say something completely inadequate like *I'm sorry*. I thought that if you were surrounded by people you would feel more at ease. But then I saw you taken."

His face contorted with sheer determination, finally getting the last knot at her legs. She jostled them free of the cord.

"Miss Lara, that woman, Alyson? She was also the same lady who told me where you were staying in Ireland," his face was grave. "I think she's likely to kill you."

He gulped, the fear touched his eyes, sending a shiver down her spine.

He was still fiddling with the ties on her hands when they heard the car pull up. Stephen focused on the knots with all of his might, trying to go faster, but Alyson had noticed the second vehicle outside the cave and came storming in.

With one look at Stephen and Beth, Alyson raised the gun and shot at them.

Elizabeth's eyes closed involuntarily.

The shot rang out into the cave.

A series of squeaks and hundreds of wings flapped together. They were suddenly surrounded by a cacophony of noise bouncing off the walls.

The bats flew past them in a wave of black, making it impossible to see anything for several seconds.

When they had cleared. Elizabeth took stock of the damage.

She couldn't feel any additional pain, but her white tank top was covered in blood. She traced it back to Stephen.

The shot had hit him in his right shoulder, inches from Beth's face.

"Jesus!" Beth screamed, moving her bound hands to his wound, applying pressure. His eyes had started to fade away. She pressed harder, trying to keep the blood in.

Alyson advanced on her, "So you were just trying to run back to Connor!"

Her eyes had gone from crazy to completely unhinged.

Beth didn't know if it was because she found them trying to escape or because she'd just shot someone, but Alyson's voice shook with the gun.

Alyson took in all the blood that now covered Elizabeth and Stephen's chests. Her eyes followed it down to the small pool on the cave floor. She took a step closer, to see what she had done.

The shot had sent a surge of adrenaline coursing through Elizabeth's veins.

Alyson took another step forward. Elizabeth watched her feet carefully, waiting for her chance.

And then she was within reach.

Elizabeth kicked her now free legs forward and to the side, sweeping Alyson's legs. It had the intended effect, Elizabeth watched as Alyson went flying backwards.

Quickly, she stole to her feet. Bending down to grab a rock between her hands, she lunged at Alyson hitting her over the head just as her fingers had closed on the gun again.

The force of it knocked Alyson's head back, the gun flew out of her hand and into the darkness of the cave beyond. Alyson laid there motionless.

Elizabeth didn't know how much time she had left, she didn't know how much time Stephen had left. She ran out of the cave blinking wildly, trying to acclimate herself to the light as soon as humanly possible.

Two cars were parked outside of the cave. The road they had driven on, wasn't even a road. It was just a path with grass and dirt, just wide enough for a compact car to squeeze through.

She considered getting in a car and trying to drive it, but her hands were still bound and her head was still pounding; her vision a blurry mess.

No, she was more likely to end up killing herself if she got behind the wheel.

She noticed the hill straight up ahead, if she could get to higher ground she would be able to tell where she was, and maybe she could find some help on the other side.

She started running as fast as her legs would take her up the dirt incline. The edge was a couple hundred feet ahead.

Just put one foot in front of the other Beth, one foot in front of the other.

She willed herself forward, finding some strength in reserve.

She didn't know if it would work, or if it was the wisest plan. She didn't know *anything*.

But she willed herself forward, hoping that her gut wouldn't fail her. She prayed to God and Mags and the Universe to help her.

To send help, to find a way out of this.

A small negative voice broke through her thoughts. *But what if there's nothing on the other side of the hill? You'll be trapped. Cornered, with no escape.*

She shook her head forcing the bad thoughts away. This was the only choice she could see. And she had to trust.

She had to trust in something.

When she was ten feet from the edge, she dropped to her knees and crawled the rest of the way.

As the edge drew nearer she could see that it wasn't a hill, it was a cliff. *No! No! No!*

She thought about going back, but she'd come this far, the least she could do was look over the side and get a sense of where she was. Maybe then another plan would present itself.

When she finally reached the edge and looked over the side, she saw that it was about thirty feet to the bottom.

Then she noticed the people.

There were people walking in the crop below. Through a vineyard.

They were walking towards the hill. She squinted trying to make out their faces.

She threw her hands over her head and waved wildly, trying to call out, *over here*! Her voice was a raspy whisper.

She pulled herself up until she was sitting on her knees and tried again, "Over here!" She used her stomach muscles to project her voice.

A man's head snapped up, seeing her.

"Help!" she wailed again.

"Lara!"

Connor.

The people started to run. As they drew closer Elizabeth could make out other faces. Her father, Brian, Matthieu, Emily, her cousins and several other people she had recently met.

They ran faster until they were at the base of the cliff, trying to visually map a way up.

But then she heard the footsteps behind her.

Slowly, Elizabeth turned to face Alyson as she closed the distance. She'd found the gun in the darkness of the cave and was now pointing it straight at her.

Again.

Alyson walked to the edge of the cliff until she was facing her.

Elizabeth tried and failed to get to her feet, all she could do was kneel and wait.

"No!" Elizabeth heard Connor scream from below.

Alyson looked over the side, seeing all the people there staring up for the first time. When she saw Connor's face, her lips twitched up into a quick involuntary smile.

The gun was firmly trained at Elizabeth's head, now just three feet from her face.

"I'm doing this for you!" Alyson yelled to Connor below. "I'm doing this for us! She was just going to leave you, she told me so. She told me that that life at your side wasn't for her. She doesn't love you like I love you, Connor. She's not what you need—I'm the one that's supposed to be your partner!"

Connor's voice changed, "*Alyson?*"

Elizabeth stole a glance below, his face was scrunched up in confusion. "Alyson *Moule?* What are you—"

And then Elizabeth watched as all the pieces fell into place. It all fit for him now, he looked up into Beth's eyes, brows drawn together in panic.

Sheer agony filled his beautiful blue eyes.

Alyson watched their exchange, and fired a shot into the air before retraining the gun back on Elizabeth's face.

"No!" Connor screamed. "No, Alyson please no! Alyson, *please!*" His voice trailed off, he was begging.

Elizabeth watched Alyson waver, hearing him say her name had affected her. But then her eyes refocused on Beth.

Elizabeth watched as her index finger closed around the trigger.

She closed her eyes, wondering what it would be like. To die.

She sent up a silent prayer, so grateful for the months that she'd had. Wondering if Mags would be there on the other side, to greet her.

She thought about how she had lost a decade. How she had spent the last several months beating herself up for it. For all of those choices.

Now at the end, she only had one regret.

That she'd never have the chance to tell Connor that he was her forever. To tell him that she couldn't wait to marry him, to start a life together. To begin their adventure.

She lowered her head and sunk to the ground whispering Connor's name as she heard the trigger tighten.

And then, Connor screamed again. "Alyson . . .! Alyson . . .!" He'd observed the effect of his saying her name, he had to try. "Alyson . . .!"

Elizabeth opened her eyes, looking down to see that Connor had crumpled to his knees.

She looked next at her assailant, Alyson had been moved by his calling out her name. So moved that she only had eyes for Connor.

Elizabeth attempted one more time, finding the last shred of life in her muscles. One final opportunity.

She tensed like a coil, preparing to explode all at once.

In one quick movement she stood up and kicked the gun out of her hand. Alyson fell to her knees with the force of the blow.

Beth managed to stay on her feet, but was now shaking violently.

Alyson begun to cry as she slumped to the floor. Elizabeth watched as the woman crumbled into a ball, broken.

And then she caught Beth's eyes.

Elizabeth readied herself, trying to step away. But Alyson launched herself, quickly and recklessly forward, trying to push them both over the cliff.

But at the very last second, in a strikingly beautiful, elegantly lithe movement, Elizabeth turned in place—it was almost a pirouette—years of muscle memory and instinct came rushing back to save her.

Alyson toppled over the side of the cliff. Beth threw her hands out to reach her, but it was too late.

She watched Alyson fall, before her own eyes closed. All the adrenaline had drained from her body as she collapsed on the edge of the small cliff.

And then the world went as dark as the cave.

CHAPTER 16: CHOOSING FOREVER

Elizabeth opened her eyes and focused on the ray of light streaming through the window of the guest master suite at Château Fleury.

She remembered collapsing on the cliff, but struggled to remember what had come later. Focusing, she tried to bring it back, until pieces of memories, flooded her brain all at once. They were blurry, erratic recollections of what had happened afterwards.

She couldn't remember how she'd gotten to Château Fleury, but she did remember the doctors, the machines, the shots. She remembered Audre and Bridgett helping her shower. She remembered Connor carrying her to the bed.

Turning onto her back, she looked up at the white ceiling. She felt someone next to her, Connor was propped up in the bed reading something on his tablet.

He felt her stir.

He dropped his tablet on the side table and sunk down in the bed until he was lying on his side facing her.

His voice was soft and sad, but he looked relieved. "Hi."

"Hi," her voice was raspy and thick with sleep.

"Stephen?" she asked, keeping her eyes trained on the ceiling.

Connor nodded gravely. "He made it. He's going to be all right. I made sure he was taken care of, don't worry."

"And Alyson?"

He shook his head. "She hit her head on a rock when she hit the bottom."

At that, Elizabeth turned back onto her side, facing the ray of light. It was unbelievably sad. The woman had nearly taken her life, but she was so very ill, Elizabeth's heart hurt thinking about how and why Alyson had met an untimely end. There was no sense to it; she remembered her kidnapper's face now, especially her eyes, wide with terror, as she realized she was going over the cliff, that she was going to die.

It gave her chills. If only Beth had reached forward a little faster. Logically, she knew she'd given every last ounce of her strength, but the loss of life weighed on her.

"How long have I been out?" she said in a serious whisper.

"Three days," his voice was filled with the same sadness.

She rested her hands beneath her cheek, focusing on the ray of light.

"Elizabeth," Connor started, "I—I . . . I'm so sorry!" His voice was filled with agony now.

The words tumbled from him, like he'd been in some fiery hell, unable to speak for three days, "Alyson, there was never anything between us. She was younger than me. In Cambridge we were all supposed to go out as a group and then I found myself alone with her and at the end of the night she tried to kiss me, but I pushed her away and told her I didn't see her that way.

"I knew that she fancied me at Cambridge, but I swear on everything that I think is holy, I never led her on. I never did anything untoward to make her feel the way she did. Clearly, she was mentally unstable, but I really need you to know that I didn't mistreat her. I didn't do anything."

She stayed silent. Letting him finish.

"I know," she said softly.

She thought he would be relieved, happy even that she didn't hold it against him. But he wasn't.

"But it didn't matter, did it?" He was in pain. "You still keep facing life and death situations because of me. Because of who I am and what was left for me. I'm terrified Lara. I'm terrified that my life will be the end of yours. I mean *Jaysus*, you've been in my life for five months and just look at what's happened."

She felt him throw his hands up into the air.

"Held at gunpoint—*twice* and drugged how many times?" he finished wildly.

He went on for several more minutes pointing out all that she'd had to go through during the course of their courtship . . . because of him. Playing the martyr, taking the blame for it all.

Elizabeth was letting him have his say. But she'd had enough. "And don't forget about the great white," she said in a flat voice.

"What?" He snapped out of his monologue of self-loathing long enough to become confused.

Her voice was light now, "If you hadn't introduced me to Fungie, then I wouldn't have been in the water with a great white shark."

A laugh bubbled up in her chest, until it forced its way out. It should have sounded odd to her ears, unnatural, something borne out of shock, but it was as light and natural as if they'd just been sitting around watching one of their eighties classics. The emotions of the last week overwhelmed her.

She started laughing in earnest, her body shaking and protesting with the force of it.

Connor put a hand on her shoulder shifting her so he could see her face.

Was she in shock? Was it possible for someone to slip into shock three days later? Did she have PTSD? His mind raced as he considered all the possibilities.

"Think all of this nearly dying business is funny?" His eyes were wide, he was not amused. He tried desperately to search her face, to figure out what was wrong with her.

"No," she said. "I think *you're* funny," she corrected. "You're hilarious, taking all of this on yourself, like it's all your fault. We all make choices Connor, and there will always be a set of variables in this life. The obsessives, the crazies, the people you piss off—all you can do is try your best from your side of the fence."

"Yes, but," he protested, "look at what you've been through . . ." he trailed off, still trying to diagnose her.

"Yeah, let's look at what I've been through. You know that first attack with Stephen, the one you blamed yourself for? If it hadn't happened and I hadn't been given the opportunity to send him to a hospital instead of a prison, he wouldn't have gotten clean, he wouldn't have felt like an ass, and he would never have come to the party looking to apologize.

"This woman, Alyson, the circumstances that brought her to that cliff, the choices—they were made way before me. She made up her mind that she was in love with you a long time ago. And she was bound to come after whomever you chose to be your partner—especially after she lost her father, which undoubtedly contributed to her instability.

"So if Stephen hadn't attacked me, he would never have come to find me and then I might not be here right now. And as for Alyson, there's another way to look at that as well.

"You see you were bound to find someone to share your life with at some point, and she might have attacked that woman like she attacked me as soon as you got serious. The difference is, *that* woman, hypothetically, let's call her *Jill*, may not have had my awesome martial arts skills through . . . or dance moves for that matter.

"And then poor Jill would have gone in my place." She raised her eyebrows, willing him to understand. "*However*," she continued, "badass that *I am*," she paused. Her voice took on a strength, a sense of ownership—the boasting brought a smile to his face, just as she'd intended, "I survived."

She took his hand, "So you could look at it this way— I'm the perfect person for you because I'm strong enough to be by your side and fight off the crazies."

He tried not to smile.

"And to tell you when you're being an ass," she added for good measure.

The bed shook then with his laughter, his relief. She wasn't in shock she was just being Lara.

His Lara.

He ran his fingers through his hair, "So does that mean you're not leaving me?" He sounded hopeful and exhausted, like he'd been certain that she would wake up and pack her bags, getting as far away from him and his life as possible.

She nodded, "That means I'm not leaving you, Connor."

Elizabeth felt him relax considerably. He let out a gust of air, letting go of some of the tension that had been trapped in his body for days.

He sunk down into the bed and rested his head against hers. He closed his eyes and a for a few minutes they remained nestled against each, neither saying a word.

Finally, he roused himself. He kissed her forehead lightly, careful not to cause her pain, and got out of the bed.

"Where are you going?" she called after him as he reached the door.

"I have to tell everyone that you're awake. They're all so worried."

She bit her lip, thoughts turning to the world and what it might have looked like in her absence, all the people she had in her life now; friends and family who cared what happened to her.

Her eyes glistened a degree as she faced the proof that she really wasn't alone in the world. She swallowed hard and successfully kept the tears from brimming over.

"Is Audre back in London?" she said quickly, thinking about her friend. How worried she'd be.

He nodded.

"OK, I think I'll give her a call then."

He turned to leave.

"But Connor?" she called again before he'd shut the door.

He stopped.

"Tell everyone I'm awake, but that I'm not ready to see anyone. Then come back, OK?"

"Yes, Miss Lara." He extended an arm and bowed, letting his lips twitch up as they often did when he executed the gesture that reminded them both of the day they'd met.

The door shut behind him.

Elizabeth got up, smoothing the cotton camisole and pajama shorts that Bridgett had lent her. She walked to the bathroom carefully, testing her limbs along the way. She ached all over, but she was desperate to brush her teeth and wash her face, to feel human again.

As she stared into the mirror and examined her face, she saw herself clearly. There were no remnants of that woman who lived in the blacks and the grays of life. Instead, she stared at the girl Mags had missed. The girl Elizabeth had missed.

It was all there, staring back at her.

This time the tears came and she didn't push them back; they streamed down her face in full force. It was a relief to cry, to realize that she'd made it all the way back, to realize that she'd become a better version of herself. She clutched the bathroom sink for support as everything became remarkably clear. Where she had been; where she was; where she wanted to go.

And she was through wasting time.

She splashed water on her face and brushed her teeth, using the blue towel on the rack to pat her face dry. Her brain worked a million miles a second, making up for lost time, until finally she decided on what to do next.

She found her phone on the side table next to the bed. Someone had thoughtfully plugged it in to charge. She picked it up and called Audre.

"Babes!" Audre answered on the second ring. She sounded so relieved. "You're alive! Oh my God, I'm so glad!"

"Yeah, I'm all better," she answered reassuringly, and then she felt the tenderness in her head and added, "Mostly."

She heard her friend breathe loudly on the other end.

Relief had rendered her normally loud and bubbly friend, speechless.

"Dree?"

"Yeah?"

"In addition to being my interior designer, best friend, maid of honor, I'm also adding wedding planner to your list. Will you do it?"

Elizabeth had expected Audre to answer instantly.

There was silence, but she could feel Dree building up to something on the other line.

"Oh yes! Yes, yes!" she shouted into the phone.

Elizabeth angled the cell away from her ear. "OK, well you've got one month, can you do it?"

"Wow! Look at you." Audre sounded impressed. "Wait, this isn't the shock talking, is it? You're not going turn into a runaway bride, are you?"

"Dree, I've never been more certain of anything in my life."

"Bloody fantastic! No problem, Babes! Eeeeek, a month. Oh my gosh this is going to be so much fun. And beautiful, just you wait and see."

The door to the bedroom opened.

"OK Dree, thanks for the help. I've got to go. Love you."

"Love you too, Liz."

Elizabeth went to sit on the bed.

"Was that Audre?" Connor asked coming to sit next to her.

She nodded with a grave face. "I have something to tell you."

Connor's face fell, he braced for the worse. "OK . . ." he said hesitantly. Anxiety coloring his blue eyes.

"When I was kneeling there on the cliff, I thought that was it. I thought that I was really going to die."

Connor stopped breathing.

"I had a regret," she continued slowly, carefully, so that he would understand that she was speaking from her soul.

He waited quietly, taking her hand in his.

"I regretted not making it clear, that you are my forever too. I want to get married and not in a year or two years like I had originally thought. I want to get married now. I've hired Audre to make it happen next month."

The corners of his mouth flickered, he was trying not to smile. "Really?" He scrunched his eyes together, searching her face, wanting desperately to believe what she was saying, but the course correction was so severe, he need to be sure. "This isn't something borne out of shock, is it? Because we don't have to decide anything, I'm perfectly happy with the way things are. I'm just ecstatic that you aren't half-way out the door."

She nodded, firm in her conviction.

He was trying not to give in to the rush of emotions that were knocking on his door, ready to break it down, ready to make him jump on a piece of furniture.

"This is something you really want?" he asked, eyes never leaving her face.

"I do," she said and smiled.

No longer capable of holding back, he gave in, letting one of his dazzling smiles reach his eyes.

"Whatever you like, Miss Lara." His eyes were bright with excitement. He leaned down to kiss her.

Their lips had only just met when her stomach growled.

"Looks like you're ready for some food. You haven't eaten in days." He turned away from her, "I'll go bring you something, just relax." He launched himself towards the door.

"Don't you dare!" She grabbed his hand, pulling him back.

"What's wrong?" He cupped her face, stroking her cheek with his thumb.

"Nothing is wrong." She leaned up and kissed him. Wrapping her hands around his neck, holding him in place.

He returned her kiss eagerly, but broke away, resting his forehead against hers. "God, I've missed you. I was so worried," he whispered.

"I'm here. I'm here," she repeated, shifting her weight backwards so he'd have to follow her onto the bed.

He brought his arms around her, holding her protectively against his side.

"You know—" he started, she cut him off with a kiss.

"Connor," she whispered against his lips, "I don't want to talk."

He finally registered the need in her eyes. She closed the distance between them an inch at a time, as he'd so often done with her.

Keeping her eyes open, she took his lips against hers, and watched as his ice blue eyes turned electric.

Hunger settled in his face. He leaned into her, positioning her on her back, carefully. He was too considerate. Too concerned about hurting her.

She reached up and brought him down on her, forcefully taking his lips, showing him that she didn't want to be treated like porcelain.

Connor broke away one final time, checking in, making sure she was all right.

Elizabeth wanted nothing more than to feel his body against hers, to be consumed by the fire.

He read the thoughts as they crossed her face, touched the part of him that wanted the same. And then there was no more deciding, he took the kit gloves off.

She smiled up at him as he gave in, coming down on her, crushing her lips in a frenzy of desperate kisses.

He'd been through hell, thinking he would lose her. *Again.* The memories all came flooding back as he moved his mouth to her neck, licking and sucking the area beneath her ear, until she giggled.

He thought it was the most glorious sound he'd ever heard.

She brought his face back to hers, opening herself up to him. Connor was relentless, losing all sense of control as he parted her lips, diving into her as deep as he could go.

He wanted to be one with her, to be entwined forever.

"Connor . . ." she whispered, as the heat settled in her body. She welcomed it, welcomed the familiar pull—the feeling of every cell in her body being awakened.

A low moan escaped her lips as he kissed her long and hard.

She reached up to remove his jeans, he couldn't wait for her to undress him. Quickly, he stood up and took off his clothes while she watched him.

When he was free, he climbed back onto the bed and kissed her stomach, using his hands to bring her sleep shorts and panties down together.

He wrapped his arms around her waist and brought her into a sitting position, moving his hands under her camisole and bringing it up over her head.

He gazed at her for a few seconds, taking her in, his expression changed from hungry to ravenous.

He threw her back onto the bed, and watched as her breasts bounced with the movement.

She smiled up at him as he shifted to his hands and knees, stalking her. Then he brought his naked body down on hers, resting there, feeling every inch of her bare skin against his.

"Connor," she whispered again.

He brought his lips back to hers, holding nothing back, devouring her at every turn.

She pulled away so she could look into his blue eyes, "Take me," she pleaded.

Connor unraveled completely as he positioned himself at her entrance and pushed himself forward.

He watched as her eyes rolled back into her head and her mouth opened in ecstasy. He drove his hips into her, letting all of his weight come down on her.

When he'd gone as far as he could go, he whispered, "I love you, Lara. The Universe sent you to me, you know." It wasn't a question.

"I know," she leaned up and kissed him.

And then they started to move together.

In that moment, nothing else existed, only their connection, their promise.

They collided into each other again and again in a manic frenzy of urgent love making. All that they had been through together, all that they had almost lost along the way, and all that they felt for each other—concentrated in one moment.

They each called out the other's name, swearing to the heavens as their bodies reached the stars.

And with one final explosion of fire, their souls were bound.

CHAPTER 17: LETTER 17

The next month passed quickly. Connor and Beth were inseparable, partly because his time was his own again and partly because he refused to leave her side.

Elizabeth teased that he was more shell-shocked than she was.

He agreed.

She read letters thirteen through sixteen during her convalescence.

Letter thirteen was a list of places Mags had wanted her to see. Letter fourteen was an SD card filled with Mags' very favorite photos, the ones that really meant something to her throughout her life. The ones she carried with her from place to place, frame to frame, wall to wall.

Letter fifteen was another SD card filled with her journals, which she'd had digitized. There were decades of memories and stories and experiences. It took Elizabeth one week complete, to read it all. But she did.

Letter sixteen was a list, *Mags' Bucket List*. It held no less than one-hundred and seventeen items.

Every single one, was crossed off.

In the end, Elizabeth Lara married Connor Bannon in a small ceremony with fifty of their closest friends and family at Château Plaisir.

Audre transformed the massive lawn into a French country-chic wedding, with a wood floor covering most of the space, framed by the manicured hedges and roses on either side.

"We are not going to put up with heels sinking in the grass." Audre had put her foot down when Beth had asked if bringing in a floor to cover the entire space was necessary. "I will not have you sinking down the aisle!"

Beth had almost opened her mouth to say that she could wear boots with her wedding gown, but Audre had thrown her a look of warning that proved she knew her friend well. It read: *don't you dare suggest that you could simply wear some comfortable, frumpy, manky old boots with your Reem Acra gown!*

The chairs were wrapped in elegant ivory silk, the aisle was adorned with lush green ivy, white lilies, and accent red roses.

The string quartet played an acoustic version of Isakov's *Second Chances.*

Connor stood with Kilian under a circular French colonnade made with white columns. He wore a black tuxedo without the bow tie. His hair was combed elegantly away from his face. His blue eyes glittered like sapphires with the sun, as he watched his beloved make her way towards him.

Elizabeth smiled at their guests as she came up after Audre, wearing a simple white gown with glistening crystals set aglow by the dying rays of the sun.

She had chosen to walk on her own, feeling both Rhia and Mags walking alongside her.

It was *their* place to accompany her—she wouldn't have anyone else.

Mona reached out and squeezed her hand, her eyes twinkled as Beth walked past.

Elizabeth nodded and smiled at Brian, her cousins, Matthieu and the rest of her family.

Loryn and Wes were both there. Wes gave her an appreciative look that would have inspired feelings of violence in Connor if he'd seen it. She bit the inside of her lip to keep from laughing.

Their friends from Ireland had made the trip as well, elated to join in their celebration.

Bram and Bree stood with Shaun, Kait, Fin, and the others, smiling from ear to ear.

Elizabeth felt a deep sense of joy, of destiny, of being in line with the Universe as her eyes met Connor's.

Somewhere in the back of her mind she was grateful she had acknowledged everyone else first as she walked down the aisle, because once her eyes locked on his, there was no looking away.

When it was time for Connor's vows, he recounted a story about a girl with long brown hair that billowed out behind her as she ran.

Over a bridge.

Something about the description, about his words felt familiar to her.

Thinking she'd already heard the story, she waited patiently for him to get to the point—to get to where he was going. To say that he loved her and pledged his life to her, as she did him.

He explained how the girl had run over a bridge and crashed into him.

Connor watched Elizabeth's face carefully as he told the story bit by bit. He was looking at her like he knew something she didn't, taking his time with it. Letting a picture form.

Suddenly, she remembered running over a bridge and crashing . . . her friends waiting to go punting . . . a mop of wild brown hair and electric blue eyes came flashing back. Elizabeth's hair stood on end, a delicious chill ran up her spine.

All those years ago . . . ?

Her jaw dropped, her head started to shake back and forth, disbelieving.

How long had he known?

Elizabeth's eyes watered as it all came rushing back and understanding dawned.

Connor's lips twitched up, reading the thoughts as they crossed her face. A deep sense of satisfaction colored his features as his Lara *finally* understood.

He came to the end, "Just call me Fate, she said . . . and so she was."

And there, before everyone they loved, they sealed their fate with a kiss, taking care to crash into each other with American zeal, Irish loyalty, and French abandon.

The chairs were cleared away, replaced by round tables. A small rectangular table was set at the head for the bride and groom. A massive dance floor took up the rest of the space.

White lights lit the hedges and roses all around the large floor. Audre had created white lattice-like structures that held plants and flowers that appeared to drip from the sky, with blue lights shining betwixt them.

Audre and Kilian's toasts as maid of honor and best man made everyone laugh. They'd taken notice of each other, joking that they were always the one in the room to say what everyone else was thinking.

Apparently, everyone was thinking that Connor and Beth were much too good looking for each other and had too much money and talent between them. Audre had started to sound like Mel B again when she proclaimed, "It's not fair!" and everyone laughed.

Kilian's toast was much in the same vein, but with more swearing, and more laughing.

Mona, now rosy with the drink, stood up. Her beautiful Irish accent became stronger with every pint. She relied on a well-known Irish toast, "May your glass be ever full. May the roof over your head be always strong."

And then as an aside, "Although these two will surely never have to worry about their roofs—how many landings do they have betwixt them now?" Mona turned to Kilian for an answer while he hid in his pint glass.

"Where was I? Eh . . . oh, right. And may you be in heaven half an hour before the devil knows you're dead." People all around laughed.

And then Mona turned serious, looking at Connor with glittering eyes, "And may Rhia be watching down on you both." She nodded with wise eyes. "She would have loved Elizabeth."

Connor and Beth both stood up to hug Mona.

Many stood to offer their congratulations, including Wes who stood with all the bravado that came with being Wes Cartwright and declared, "Here's to the nights we'll never remember with the friends we'll never forget." He raised his glass.

Then continued as people took their requisite drinks, "And may Connor Bannon never forget that, should he ever falter . . . others will be only too eager to take his place." He gave Elizabeth a wicked grin and a wink.

"Wes!" she looked at him shocked, but with a smile on her face.

Connor laughed, nodding at Wes. "Oh, it's all in good fun, Lara." Connor stood up and the two men shook hands, heartily. Laughing together.

Connor patted Wes on the shoulder with a, "Good man." Then came back to their table. "Besides," he winked as he sat down next to her, "I'll never forget." He leaned in for a kiss.

Matthieu stood up just then, clinking his glass to get everyone's attention, "Lizzie . . . my Lena, your Mags," he nodded, once everyone had fallen silent, "is here with you now." His eyes crinkled with emotion, his accent became more British with every glass of champagne.

"She would be so proud of you. Proud of the journey you took, proud of the ending you fought for, proud of the life you've crafted. Knowing and loving her for as long as I did, I can say with absolute certainty, that she would have thoroughly enjoyed Connor."

He turned to the other guests, gesturing with his hands, "This all feels . . . *destined* somehow. Treasure your moments, my darlings. The ones like tonight, the ones that seem written in the stars, will light your way, if properly cared for up here," he tapped a finger to his temple.

"Tonight, I say we dance under the stars and take in their light, because as we all know, their light," he pointed up, "will continue shining long after we've shuffled off this mortal coil."

He turned back to Beth, "Congratulations, my Darling. May your new life be as bright as the stars."

The wedding party erupted in appreciative applause, with the sound of clinking glasses and *Cheers! Salud! Santé!* and *Sláinte!* all being exchanged simultaneously.

After the toasts there was dancing. The music was the only part of the affair that Elizabeth had insisted on maintaining complete control.

She'd never imagined her own wedding; had never thought or dreamed about it, but she had always known what music would be playing.

And so the sets varied from folk, to French country ballads, to Henry Mancini and Frank Sinatra, to Katy Perry, Lady Gaga, Queen, and Bon Jovi.

Connor took her hand and led her to the center of the floor as the opening notes of Edith Piaf's *La Vie En Rose* started to play.

"Heeey," she said to Connor as he drew her into his arms. "How'd that get in there?"

"I thought you liked Edith Piaf?" Connor mused.

"I do, but this song didn't make the list!"

Connor whispered at her ear, "Why not, Lara? Is it too sappy for you?" His voice tickled her.

She laughed, "No, I just prefer, *Non, Je Ne Regrette Rien.* Plus, it's more in keeping with the year's theme."

"Is that right?" he laughed softly.

The music swelled and the classic melody took over. They swayed back and forth, lost in each other's arms, lost in the lights, the stars, the love.

She watched as Matthieu took Mona for a spin. Although, the years and her children had made her short and round, she moved gracefully. The years she'd spent as a dancer had not left her.

The music changed, Elizabeth watched as her friends and family mixed together on the floor. Gratified by all of the dancing and laughter.

Wes seemed to hit it off with Bree and Bridgett both, but had taken the last several songs with Bridgett—her cousin had her powers of flirtation turned on high. Elizabeth watched as Wes started to fall under her spell.

She bit the inside of her lip, worried for her friend, as she danced in her husband's arms.

Bridgett was exactly Wes' type. Beautiful, French, and lethal.

But then the song ended, and Wes shook his head, seeming to snap out of it. He removed Bridgett's arms from around his neck as the next song played.

Elizabeth tuned in to hear him turn her down, "French *and* a blood relative of Elizabeth Lara? I don't think I would survive!"

He left her pouting in her short black dress in the middle of the floor, choosing instead to throw an arm around Bree, bringing her out and holding her close.

Elizabeth took turns dancing with Kilian and Matthieu and Alexandre.

She thanked Kilian for being such a good friend to them both. She thanked Matthieu for his toast and for being her family.

She thanked her father for his wedding gift. He'd chosen to give her *L'Amour*, the piece she'd admired at his show. It now stood as the centerpiece of the great entrance hall in Château Plaisir, surrounded by Audre's carefully crafted designs.

Near the end of the night, when everyone could be found on the dance floor, Brian took Beth and Connor aside.

He led them up towards the small grove of trees, at the back of her property. She hadn't yet explored anything beyond the massive lawn.

Although they'd left the lights of the party below, their steps were lit by the radiant lavender light of the full moon.

The balmy night had turned breezy, and Connor walked with his arm protectively around her shoulders.

When they reached the clearing, Brian stepped aside, revealing four white marble headstones that captured the moonlight in much the same way that her favorite sculpture at the Louvre did.

Elizabeth went automatically, sinking down to the grass.

Brian stood behind her and explained. Mags had special instructions for her remains. She had instructed him to have her cremated, but she was also to have a burial for her friends to grieve.

"She left explicit instructions, some of her ashes are buried under this headstone and the rest are here," Brian walked behind the stone and extracted a small urn.

He handed it to her.

"She would like her remains to be scattered at the Cliffs of Moher. Preferably, now this is verbatim: *with the Eagles or the Beatles playing in the background.*"

Elizabeth laughed through her tears. She set the ashes down in front of her and looked at the other graves.

Brian followed her gaze explaining. The other three headstones were for her mother Carolina, her grandmother Aurora, and Elsa.

Brian explained that Mags had them all moved there some years before, when she first bought the place.

Elizabeth let Brian's words sink in. She took several blades of grass between her fingers as she thought about her loved ones.

The men stood behind her. They let the grove fall silent, letting only the sound of the beetles and the birds pierce the space, giving the departed their proper moment.

And then Elizabeth remembered letter seventeen.

She had tucked it into her bra, a tribute to Mags herself, who often hid special treasures in her brassiere. It was also her something *old*.

And there, kneeling on the grass in her simple white wedding gown that glittered with the moonlight, Elizabeth opened the final letter.

Dear Lizzie,

I hope these letters have taken you on an extraordinary adventure. A glorious journey of self-discovery, and friends, and love. It was my honor to watch you grow into the astounding woman you are today. I'll always be in your heart, my Lizzie.

My last piece of advice is this: fill your life with as many friends, and adventures, and as much love as possible. I promise that in the end, you will leave with no regrets.

Until we meet again.

Love,
Mags

Epilogue: On the Horizon

The sky cleared on the Cliffs of Moher after a day of heavy rains.

Elizabeth stood on the edge of the cliff, watching the sunset, hugging the simple silver urn.

And so Elizabeth and Magdalen finally made it to the Cliffs together, with a contingent of family and friends standing guard behind them.

Brian, Matthieu, Audre, Wes, Emily, Renée, Liliane, Bridgett, Alexandre, Kilian, Bree, and Mona were all there bearing witness.

When the sun had nearly set, Elizabeth opened the urn.

Behind her, Kilian started to play a mashup of the Eagles' *Hotel California* and the Beatles' *In My Life* on his guitar.

Sending her love and good wishes and thanking her great-aunt for stacking the deck as she had so aptly put it in that first letter, Elizabeth sent Mags off on her last great adventure.

She reached out and took Connor's hand as the last of the golden rays disappeared over the horizon.

. . .

Sometime later, when Elizabeth and Connor traveled to Tibet, he looking for a holy relic, and she taking photographs for her upcoming show in London, she remembered something.

"Connor," she ventured as they curled up together for warmth in the small valley atop the mountain.

He nuzzled her cheek as she stared up at the clear night sky. "Yes, Lara?"

"Do you remember when we were first in Ireland and you were heading to the airport, leaving for Africa?"

He nodded, waiting for her to finish.

"You kissed me and then you whispered something in Gaelic."

She felt his chest stir with a laugh.

"Yes, go on," he prodded.

"I asked you what it meant. . . ."

"I remember," he mused. "I said goodbye *mo shíorghrá, chífidh mé i Londain thú*," he repeated.

"You said that you would tell me one day, is that day today?"

She waited.

She could hear his smile.

"Loosely translated, I said goodbye my soulmate, I'll see you in London."

She considered that, "So then you were always planning on following me to London." It wasn't a question.

"Yes, Luv. Since first I saw your gorgeous green eyes in Cambridge, I was prepared to follow you to the ends of the Earth."

"Fate," she repeated simply.

"Fate." He nodded.

They leaned into each other for a kiss as the meteor shower began.

Their eyes were turned skyward as the sparkling lines of fire lit the black night, chasing the horizon.

THE END.

A NOTE FROM JULES

If you enjoyed *The Irish Cottage*, *The London Flat*, and *The Paris Apartment*, please leave reviews. I spent a year working on this trilogy—hoping that my words would delight and entertain . . . and maybe even inspire.

But without reviews, books can fall into obscurity in an instant. So please, take a moment to show me some love.

Remember, the words you attach to my books serve as little pieces of gold that make those Amazon book pages shine brighter. That sounds so sappy, I know, but what can I say—this is the end of Elizabeth & Connor's story, and I'm feeling kind of sappy. I've enjoyed living in their world and I'm sad to leave.

But life moves on . . . to Scotland. I hope to see you all there. Join the Readers Group—it's like booking your ticket for our next adventure together.

♥ With a grateful heart, Jules ♥

In case you missed the Bonus Scene Preview at the end of *The London Flat*, here's the entire Scene for your reading pleasure. It is exclusive to the Readers Group and to this print edition of the *The Paris Apartment*. Read on for *Elizabeth & Connor Take a Tour of the Harry Potter Film Studio*. .
. .

THE
London
FLAT

DELETED SCENE

JULIET
GAUVIN

DELETED/BONUS SCENE: Elizabeth & Connor Take A Tour of the Harry Potter film Studio

The following scene was deleted because it didn't quite fit within the timeline of the book. It takes place sometime after the ending of *The London Flat*, but the scene exists independently from the story (except for the fact that Connor and Elizabeth are now together). For more bonus content join The Readers Group by going to Jules' website:

www.julietgauvin.com.

. . .

They'd only let go of each other briefly to take showers sometime late that morning. And even then they hadn't been apart for very long, since Connor jumped in twenty minutes into Beth's shower.

She'd been standing there, letting the water hit her neck, her shoulders, and cascade down her back, when the glass door opened.

After so many weeks apart, both of them felt the strong pull to keep within reaching distance of one another. It was less a desire and more a need.

They'd spent the day in bed mostly, only emerging from their love nest long enough to order pizza and for about a half an hour when Beth had insisted Connor come sit with her on the bench in Rose Square.

That evening, Connor procured a car and told her that he had a surprise. She'd looked at him wearily, thinking that no surprise could be better than spending more time curled up next to him on the couch opposite the Chagall or upstairs in bed. But she agreed to go along because the mischievous glint in his blue eyes was so very endearing.

And because he said she could go in jeans and a T-shirt.

The one-hour drive through the countryside, passing the green hills and picturesque villages, reminded her how much, on the whole, England reminded her of a storybook.

Connor held her hand and let her drift off to sleep as the thatched roof cottages started blurring against the rolling green hills and the setting sun.

He roused her some time later when the sky was dark. He'd pulled over to the side of the road and made her put on a blindfold for the last mile. Still drowsy and barely awake, she'd let him.

Five minutes later, the car had come to a full stop, he'd taken her by the hand and lead her across gravel that crunched under her feet, through a set of doors, into a foyer, and then finally through a set of very large doors that creaked with grandeur.

She could tell the doors were large through the blindfold, not just because of the creak, but because the room beyond them must have had a very tall ceiling. Elizabeth felt a distinct lack of obstruction in the air over her head.

The clack of her boots also echoed slightly against the walls. The room was completely silent except for the sound of their steps. It smelled old, musty, and new at the same time.

"Ready, Lara?" Connor's voice was a low whisper in her ear.

Her lips twitched up involuntarily as he said her name. Their reunion was so new that hearing the adoration in his voice every time he said her name like that, like a caress, still thrilled her.

Saying her name without holding his love for her back, gave him a similar thrill.

Her voice was still thick from her nap, "Yes," she nodded at the same time.

He removed the blindfold, and the familiar twinkling notes of the main Harry Potter theme swelled as her eyes calibrated to the scene in front of her.

She was standing in the Great Hall at Hogwarts. Long tables set with shining plates and goblets stood ready for Harry and the gang to come marching through the doors.

Beth's hands flew to her mouth. Almost as soon as the music had started and her eyes adjusted to the space, she'd started giggling like a child. After a moment she doubled over and put her hands on her knees, letting her laughter bellow out and fill the Hall.

Her eyes moved this way and that, taking in every detail she could, quickly, as if the beautiful mirage might disappear at any moment. Still laughing she clasped her hands under her chin and started bouncing up and down in place.

Connor laughed then, too. "I take it this is a *good* surprise, then?"

She glanced at him only for a second, but she reached for his hand and gave it a squeeze, then dragged him towards the Gryffindor table. "How did you *do* this?" she asked with more than a little awe in her voice.

They were completely alone, the studio was clearly closed to the public, but somehow they were inside. "Wait, don't tell me—you know a guy."

He chuckled, "Not this time Lara. I'm connected, but it's not like I 'ave a guy in every corner." He tried to sound shocked by her assumption, but he only succeeded in sounding more Irish.

"Then?" she asked, looking up. The flying candles were missing, replaced instead with track lighting rigged to the ceiling.

"I don't know a guy, I *bribed* a guy. There's a difference." He corrected, back straightening.

Elizabeth whistled low, thinking about how much it must have cost. "So we're really alone, then?"

"Just us and the maintenance lad I bribed to put the lights and music on." He winked at her, "We've got the whole place to ourselves, Luv."

She looked at him then, smiling brightly. His face mirrored her delight, except his eyes. His eyes were filled mostly with glee, but the hunger touched them for an instant.

The music swelled then, the fluttering trills crescendoed into the big orchestral theme. She dropped his hand and climbed over the golden rope, throwing one leg over the bench and then the other.

She sat there, looking up and down the long table imagining what it might be like if house-elves really were standing in the identical hall that would have existed just beneath her feet, ready to snap their fingers and make the feast appear in front of her.

There were headless mannequins along the walls that held Gryffindor house robes. The other houses were represented as well. Costumes that the actors had worn in the films, no doubt.

Gargoyles and dragons and snakes and ravens were mounted alongside the windows. Chains attached to bowls of fire, hung from their mouths.

She glanced towards the front of the Hall at the teacher's table. The robes of Professor Flitwick, Mad-Eye Moody, Professor Trelawney, and Professor McGonagall stood to the left of Professor Dumbledore's golden podium.

The mannequin sporting Dumbledore's robes stood just in front of the owl lectern. Professor Snape, Hagrid, and Filch's robes stood to the right.

Suddenly taken by an idea, Elizabeth, climbed back over the rope and sprinted through the massive empty space between the long tables, towards Dumbledore and the lectern. Her hair billowed out wildly behind her.

"Lara?" Connor called after her.

She stopped just before reaching another yellow rope, swinging her legs over and climbing the two steps onto the platform. Carefully, she maneuvered herself between mannequin Dumbledore and the gold podium.

Connor chuckled, "Wha—what, are ya' doin'?"

Elizabeth stood up straight and faced the Hall, pretending she was about to give a grand speech.

She cleared her throat and placed her hands on either side of the lectern.

"Welcome . . . to another year at Hogwarts," she said in her best British accent.

Connor doubled over, his hands on his knees. Beth had never heard him laugh quite that uncontrollably. It was infectious.

"Sh—shh," her voice cracked as she tried not to laugh. "The coming months, will undoubtedly—" Connor howled louder than before, practically falling to the floor.

She gave up and stood there laughing with him. When they were both good and finished, she closed her eyes and imagined what it would be like if it were all real.

If there really was magic in the world. Then she thought of the last several months and realized, she'd gotten pretty close. Mags' letters felt like magic, Lough Rhiannon too, and the million little things that had happened along the way.

Standing in the clearing with Connor, looking up at the stars after that first meal at O'Leary's. Dancing under string lights at the food festival, making love in front of the lake under the full moon after narrowly escaping death. Seeing the bauble Rhia had left for Connor on his treasure hunt sitting in the small box at the Natural History Museum. Running after him after winning Wildlife Photographer of the Year . . . Fungie.

When she opened her eyes, Connor was there a few feet in front of her, an adoring look on his face. Her stomach dropped to her feet. Would she ever get used to him looking at her like that?

She smiled back at him and turned to move off the podium, forgetting about mannequin Dumbledore just inches behind her.

She slammed straight into the costume, knocking it over; he was so fast, she barely saw him move. Connor leapt over the ropes and threw his arms out, catching it before it hit the ground.

It looked like Connor was dipping Dumbledore. He tilted his head up and caught her eyes, seeing the humor in the situation.

Together they righted the prop. He extended his arm. She took his hand, successfully sidestepping down from the raised platform. "Whoops!" she smiled at him as he rolled his eyes and bit back a grin.

"Come on there, Luv. Before you break something and it costs me some real money. And how would I explain that? I apologize, you see, my gurlfriend fancied herself Dumbledore and accidentally knocked the poor sod right off of his pedestal?"

She looked at him seriously, "Don't joke about Dumbledore! It's sacrilegious." She pursed her lips and narrowed her eyes.

His mouth dropped, "I wouldn't dream of it, Luv!" he teased.

He held out a hand like he was helping her out of a carriage, she took it and went back to the legal side of the rope.

Connor brought her hand up to the crook of his elbow as they strolled down the center of the Hall. "So Lara, in which house would the Sorting Hat have placed you?"

"Gryffindor, obviously." Then she stopped to think. "Well . . . I guess I was born a Gryffindor with Ravenclaw leanings, turned Slytherin for a decade, and now I'm back where I belong." She nodded decisively. It was a strange comfort to clear up her Hogwarts House affiliation. "And you?"

Connor stared straight ahead towards the massive doors to the Hall, thinking. "Oh I s'pose I'm a Gryffindor with a Hufflepuff mother and a demon Slytherin father." His mood turned serious, the way it always did when he mentioned them. "So the other two houses are in my blood somewhere."

Elizabeth squeezed his arm, breaking him out of the dark place he sometimes went to when he considered whether he might have inherited some power-control hungry instinct from his father, along with the castle.

She smiled up at him encouragingly, letting it touch her eyes so he might see that she didn't believe Connor could have any part of that man running through him. He'd always been kind and considerate to everyone around him, not selfish and possessive.

There only seemed to be one trigger for his perceived dark side, and that was Elizabeth. Her life, her safety, and judging by his reaction to her old friend and recent romantic suitor, Wes Cartwright, her affection as well.

He brought his other hand up to cover hers as they walked silently out of the Hall.

They passed the exhibit on writing the screenplays, the costume exhibit dedicated to The Goblet of Fire, Elizabeth had once again gone over the rope to take Hermione's pink-lavender dress between her fingers, bringing her hand down on Harry's dress robes as she stepped away.

There were millions of artifacts from animatronics to more costumes and the Mirror of Erised and the Portrait of the Fat Lady.

Elizabeth settled herself on the brown couch with deep-red blankets strewn across it, opposite the stone fireplace in the Gryffindor common room. Connor joined her.

He reached for her knees and brought her legs across his lap. He looked straight ahead where the flames might have been.

Beth curled her knees and scooted into him until she was wrapped around his side, her cheek on his shoulder. "What are you thinking?"

He tilted his head, his brow furrowed. A look of uncertainty colored his features.

"What?" She poked at his ribs. "Tell me."

A wicked half grin transformed his face, "I'm thinkin' that I wish we could apparate back to your bed." The hunger touched his eyes.

She bit her lip, completely affected by that look he sometimes gave her—like he wanted to devour her right then and there. Which of course, he did.

She moved completely into his lap. "Well, you know we could make out like naughty teenagers staying out past curfew, right here." Her voice dropped an octave.

He bit the inside of his lip and brought one hand to cradle her face, his thumb grazed her bottom lip. "I s'pose we could." His Irish accent was thick.

He closed the distance, plying her lips open with his, moving with the authority of a man who knew exactly what he wanted.

Her fingers clawed playfully into his hard chest. He moved his lips down to her neck, licking, kissing and sucking as he went.

"Did you ever imagine," he said between kisses, "that one day you would be holed up here, playing make believe at Hogwarts with a dashing Irishman who is completely under your spell?"

She laughed a little, he increased the pressure of his mouth on her neck. "Ahh. . . .." She tried and failed to answer. "Shut up." She moved his head back to hers and shifted her body until she was straddling him.

He sunk back into the couch and brought his hands down to her hips.

At that moment, the music swelled all around them, back to the main orchestral theme. It brought her back down to reality.

Sitting up, she pulled away from their kiss. "How long did you say we have until we have to leave?"

He took one hand from her hip and reached into his pocket, extracting his cell phone. "Let's see . . . it closed to the public at eight, we got here at nine thirty, and have until eleven."

He looked back into her face.

"And . . . ?" she prodded. "What time is it now?"

"Ten fifteen."

"Arghh!" She moved off of him. "Come on let's go, I love kissing you, but I really don't want to miss out on the rest of this." She motioned with her hands. "You did go through all that trouble, after all."

They rose from the couch, ready to continue exploring.

They found their way through the other exhibits. One on special effects, another specifically on chocolate, one on wigs and makeup. They looked at part of the marble staircase, and the great wall of Umbridge edicts, and the giant clock.

When they came upon the Boys' Dormitory and five four-posters with deep-red velvet curtains, the mere sight of the beds created an instant electric charge between them.

They weren't even touching, but both took a decisive step away from each other. Elizabeth moved quickly out of the room. *No way was she going to make out with Connor on or near Harry's bed.* Talk about sacrilegious. . . .

They saw Snape's potions classroom where a cauldron sat on a table, glowing red and stirring itself. And there was the Phoenix staircase to Dumbledore's Office, and then Dumbledore's Office.

Elizabeth got goose bumps standing there, in front of his desk. Looking up at the stacks upon stacks of bookcases, and the portraits of the sleeping headmasters, and the cases of odd gleaming trinkets that were undoubtedly objects of great magical power.

There was Hagrid's flying motorcycle, and Lupin's classroom, and Hogsmeade Village. The House Cup and the Goblet of Fire.

An exhibit on animal actors and Hagrid's Hut complete with Fang and a life-size, albeit headless, Hagrid mannequin.

There was the kitchen from The Burrow, a pair of knitting needles making a scarf, an iron ironing a shirt, and a pan washing itself.

They went outside briefly to see the twenty-two foot tall Knight Bus, Tom Riddle's Grave, and Privet Drive. When they came to the Hogwarts bridge which Seamus Finnigan had been charged with blowing up in the last film, Connor took her hand.

They finished the outdoor exhibits holding hands contentedly, but as soon as they stepped back into the confines of the studio, that same charge that threatened to have them take off their clothes and go at it where they stood, returned.

Elizabeth dropped his hand and for the next ten minutes walked a few feet in front of him.

They looked up in awe at all the goblin masks and mermaids and dragons' heads and thestrals in the Creature Shop. There was a glass box where a moving Hedwig stood and the small Voldemort like creature that had laid dying in King's Cross in the last film curled up and moved its head. Dementors and Aragog hung from the ceiling while Buckbeak sat on its legs and looked at you curiously.

She could feel Connor's eyes on her from behind. They pulled at her, willed her to turn around and give in. Her chest rose and fell quickly as she walked in front of him down

Diagon Alley, barely registering Ollivander's and the other colorful shops that lined the walkway.

Finally, they came across the giant model of Hogwarts. It stood almost twenty feet in the air and was nearly fifty feet in diameter. The sign said it was a 1:24 scale model.

The lights inside the castle flickered and changed. Over the course of four minutes they watched as the turreted Gothic castle went through a day-to-night cycle. Along with the music providing the ever important soundtrack, the effect was spectacular.

Connor came up on her side. Their bare arms grazed each other, sending an electric shock up and down her body. Parts of her dropped in delicious waves.

Instinctively, she looked around for cameras.

Connor felt it too, and after a minute couldn't hold back any longer.

He grabbed her hand and pulled her flush against him. He leaned in to kiss her, but she arched her back so he couldn't bridge the distance. She knew if they started they wouldn't be able to stop.

Connor's voice was low, husky, "Let's go back to Dumbledore's Office and have a snog." It was practically a whisper.

She scrunched her nose, in spite of what her body was telling her.

He searched her face, "Sacrilegious?"

She nodded, eyes wide. They couldn't do that in *Dumbledore's* space!

"Alright, then." He looked away. Resigned, he released her. Then he turned back suddenly, "What about Umbridge's Office? We didn't cover the whole tour—I hear it's around here somewhere." The mischief touched his blue eyes.

Her eyebrows drew together as she thought through his proposal. Then, with a decisive nod, "Done," she said and took his hand.

They sped out of the room to find a more appropriate place.

When they were halfway there, Connor stopped under a Gothic arch. He turned and brought her into him, wrapping his arms around her waist and lodging his right hand in the back pocket of her jeans.

He let his forehead rest against hers, stilling them both for a long moment. Their chests rose and fell in unison. He stared at her until all she could see were the blues of his eyes. They were like great big crystal pools.

Finally, he opened his mouth. The words were slow, deliberate . . . beautiful. "I love you, Lara."

Her lips turned up into a big goofy grin as he closed the distance.

. . .

Join The Readers Group For Future Bonus Content & Exclusive Giveaways

www.julietgauvin.com

ACKNOWLEDGEMENTS

This book would not have been possible without my Unicorn, my Yeti, and my Dragon. Oh yeah . . . and my family!

Thanks also for the support, inspiration, and moxie of the YWLA Writers Group.

Finally, to all my friends: the ones I've lost and the ones I'll meet this year.

PSA: Many bananas, crackers and vats of Earl Grey were consumed in the making of this trilogy.

ABOUT THE AUTHOR

Juliet is originally from California. She is a true, hopeless, all-in romantic. Her first kiss was with a Frenchman in Paris, her first love was an Eagle Scout, and her first crash-and-burn was with someone from Harvard (Jules studied history at Yale—she should have known better). When she isn't writing she can be found photographing landscapes, binge-watching entire series on Netflix, or dancing the international cha-cha.

The Paris Apartment was inspired by her time living in France.

She loves the Irish, but she loves the Brits as well. Her dream isn't a house on Maui, although she would be perfectly accepting of such a gift from the Universe; her dream is a London flat, and maybe one in Dublin, and one in Edinburgh. Can you guess where her next series might be set?

Titles by Juliet Gauvin

The Irish Heart Series (Complete)

The Irish Cottage: Finding Elizabeth (BOOK 1)

The London Flat: Second Chances (BOOK 2)

The Paris Apartment: Fated Journey (BOOK 3)

FOR RELEASE DATES, BONUS
CONTENT & EXCLUSIVE GIVEAWAYS
JOIN THE READERS GROUP:

WWW.JULIETGAUVIN.COM

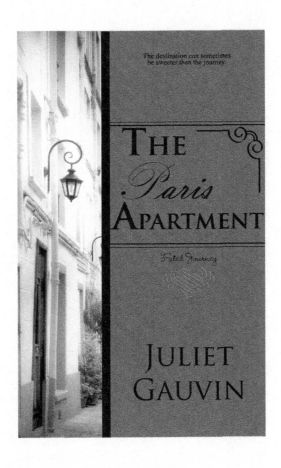

CARPE DIEM

My Bucket List:

CPSIA information can be obtained
at www.ICGtesting.com
Printed in the USA
LVOW03s1921280917
550088LV00001B/7/P